Hidebound

Joy V. Smith

Published by Joy V. Smith, 2011.

This is a work of fiction. Similarities to real people, places, or events are entirely coincidental.

HIDEBOUND

First edition. August 18, 2011.

Copyright © 2011 Joy V. Smith.

ISBN: 979-8224231225

Written by Joy V. Smith.

Hidebound

by

Joy V. Smith

Hidebound

Fissa paused to listen before turning the corner. You learn more with your mouth shut and your mind open, Uncle Torvil had often told her. The "Corridor Closed, Use The Core Elevator," sign hadn't deterred her. This corridor was a shortcut to Cat's Cave; she was curious, and since she was related to the captain, she might get away with it.

"Gotta be an android. Snark said the bullets just bounced off him, and he'd stove in his skull with an arm while Snark was still going for his gun."

"He's certainly fast then, 'cause Snark's good. That's why the captain assigned him to Koss. He don't care about other people's fusses, but he don't want nothing to happen on his ship that he didn't order it to happen. Anyone know anything about the assassin?"

"Came aboard at the last stop. Hope he's the only one The Combine sent. 'Cause Old Nordic ain't going to stop till he or Koss is dead. I admire Koss' guts for trying to take over The Combine, but I don't want them all over the ship. This mess is bad enough."

His companion grunted assent. When the silence continued, Fissa rounded the corner. Two crewmen were assiduously working on one bone-white wall; they'd finished the floor, which gleamed wetly, making it a darker green. She saw in a glance that the scrub water was a deep and dirty pink.

The man closest to her looked up with a frown as he glimpsed an intruder, but the frown turned into a smile when he recognized her. "Sorry, Miss Skarvan," he said, respectfully but firmly. "This corridor is closed. You must have missed the sign." They all knew she hadn't.

Fissa flashed him a confiding smile. "I was planning to den up in The Cave, Franco," she said. "This way is much quicker." She smiled again, being sure to include the other crewman, Olas.

Franco shook his head. "I don't fancy my hide up on the Captain's trophy wall," he said softly. "You'd best run along now."

Olas had looked willing enough, Fissa noticed, until Franco mentioned the trophy wall. Then he'd turned quickly back to his work. "What happened, Franco?" she asked. It was worth a try.

He shook his head again and waited pointedly for her to leave. She left, disappointed, but she knew Captain Saknusson ran a tight ship. That was why she'd booked passage on the St. Catherine. The captain was her mother's cousin, and Fissa had heard her speak of him with affection and respect. If her mother thought she was safe on his ship, maybe she wouldn't worry and have her shipped back home, as had happened twice before. With so many worlds to explore, she didn't want to be stuck on one planet the way her mother had been.

Fissa went straight to the purser's office. She was sure Fortsworth couldn't keep quiet if his life depended on it. St. Catherine was not a state-of-the-art passenger ship, catering to the rich and famous. That was one reason Fissa enjoyed getting to know practically everyone on the ship—crew and passengers alike. Her innate curiosity was another.

"Do you know about Koss?" Fortsworth asked cautiously, glancing sideways in all directions—so anxiously that Fissa feared she wouldn't learn much. She needn't have worried.

"Yes," she whispered, leaning forward across the counter. They were at the far end, away from the door. Fortsworth kept one pale blue eye glued to his monitor as he talked.

"Koss came aboard with four bodyguards, but the captain assigned him to Snark anyway. There's one, however, that Koss relies on; his name is Ferenc, and he seems to be from some backwater planet. He speaks galactic hardly at all; in fact, he rarely says anything. We're sure everything is new to him—because he's made some strange mistakes, but he's real cool about it. And he concentrates completely on Koss—as if he's the center of his universe."

"Sounds like an android to me," Fissa said when the purser stopped for a breath.

"Nope. Androids have to be registered, and the captain did a check as soon as he could after he first saw him. He's a strange one all right, but he's humanoid. Captain Saknusson's careful. Koss fought him over the tests, but the Captain said he couldn't stay aboard if he didn't command the man to submit. And we were a long way out of port when he said it." Fortsworth snickered.

"What did the tests show?"

"No one knows." Fortsworth was clearly disappointed at not being able to tell her. "But the captain sent a coded message to our next stop—Mozartt."

"I met Koss once," Fissa said thoughtfully. "That was enough—short and stocky as I recall, but, despite that, he's quick and has a good reach. He was alone then, though."

"Looks that way sometimes when he's on the prowl," Fortsworth said in a warning tone. "Best avoid him."

Fissa thought there was obviously more he could tell. "I'd like to see Ferenc for myself," she said. Is here any time I can catch him alone?"

"No!"

After some fruitless prowling and delicate questioning of other crew members, Fissa decided to stake out the dining room and wait until Koss' party appeared. She'd discovered they didn't eat during regular hours, but she had the time and money, so she amused herself by working her way through the menu. Some things she didn't even consider tasting, but she let them run loose on the table and nibble at the food she had left on her plate.

When the serving staff attempted to shift her out of the dining room she refused to go. "I haven't finished," she told Paul, looking at him with puzzled, dark hazel eyes. She indicated her plate, with a long, elegant finger and its polished silver nail. Eventually he gave up, shrugged, and finished his shift, leaving her alone in the room. Fortunately, he didn't report her to the captain, the only thing she worried about.

Late that night, she considered her next move. She wasn't about to give up, but she had to take a break, she reluctantly admitted to herself. Even she couldn't ignore the demands of nature. She rose, hesitated a minute, wondering what to do with the little creatures still on her table. While most of them had gone to sleep, a couple appeared to be looking for a way to escape.

Then movement in the doorway caught her attention, and she looked up. A man was standing just inside the door, studying her. She didn't move. He was obviously an advance scout. She was sure it was Ferenc. His quiet stillness was alien in a way that intrigued her. He was a few inches taller than she—not quite six feet. His skin was much darker than her own—a golden brown; and his hair was short and tight to his scalp and the same color as his skin. He had wide-set, thick-lidded, orange eyes.

Fissa observed all this in the long moments he studied her. As she stood up, breathing was the only movement she dared to make. She was sometimes reckless, but not stupid. Then Snark arrived.

"It's all right," he said. "This is Miss Skarvan. She is not a threat." He moved forward until he was standing between them. "Come along, Miss Skarvan. The room is reserved at this time. You'll have to leave."

Fissa accompanied him out the door. "Thank you," she said, turning to him when they were in the hall.

Snark, glancing beyond her, stiffened. "Go now," he demanded, as he stepped a few paces ahead of her.

"Anfissa Skarvan, isn't it?" a fondling sort of voice said.

Fissa turned to see Varn Koss. His grizzled blond hair and beard were almost as oily as he sounded. As he moved in on her, she shifted to keep Snark between them.

Koss was just as quick as she remembered, and somehow she ended up against the wall, with Koss not quite touching her. Snark was shoved aside by the other bodyguard, a big man with a leering expression on his long face. Ferenc joined them, but stood apart, watching dispassionately.

"Why don't you join me for supper?" Koss asked.

Fissa shook her head, but managed a slight smile. "I had a late supper myself," she said. "Another time perhaps."

Koss pressed. "Tomorrow night?"

"Perhaps," she said and slipped sideways, brushing past Ferenc, who was now flanking Koss' other side. She heard a grunt behind her, but didn't risk looking back until she'd reached the corner. A quick glance revealed the big bodyguard was glaring at Ferenc. Koss and Snark were ignoring them and walking away.

She went straight to her suite. Tomorrow she'd ask Snark what had happened. She sighed as she remembered her half-promise to Koss. It'd been the surest way to escape though.

The next day, Fissa persuaded Fortsworth to help her find Snark. She learned that he went off duty after the usual late supper, then reported back to Koss sometime the following afternoon. Fissa found Snark eating a belated breakfast, alone in the crew's mess hall.

"You're worse than a cable weevil for getting into places you shouldn't," he muttered. He pointed a brown finger to a seat opposite, and asked if she wanted anything to eat.

"I don't plan to eat for at least a week," she said. "What I need to know is—what happened after I took off last night?"

Snark's deep brown eyes narrowed. "That's a good question," he replied, giving her a serious look. "Pounder grabbed for you. Either he figured Koss wasn't finished with you, or he was just using that as an excuse to grab you; but Ferenc got in his way and wouldn't budge. I haven't the faintest idea why he did it. Usually he doesn't make a move without Koss' say-so. Koss acted like he hadn't noticed a thing."

"It was probably just an accident."

"Probably," Snark said. "But I've got to warn you—stay away from Koss. He's a pervert. He watches things I never would have believed." He looked away, as if he didn't want her to see in his eyes even a hint of the things he'd seen.

"I intend to avoid him," she reassured him. And she meant it. She spent the whole night in her suite, with tapes from home . She started out with the tape of Wodenhouse plant life her mother had given her on her last birthday. She was admiring a hybrid of the rain lily—brought from Terra generations ago—and which she looked forward to seeing there, when her door squealed open.

It was Ferenc! How had he forced his way through a door that was electronically locked, and made to resist nothing less than a laser or a bomb? "Koss waits for you," he said.

"I'm not coming tonight," she replied. Start as you mean to go on, her mother had told her. She stood up, pushing the chair back so it was between them. Immediately she felt incredibly foolish.

It took him less than a second to cross the room, brush the chair out of the way, and pick her up. He was almost out the door with her when she demanded he stop. "I have to get dressed. I can't go with you this way. Captain Saknusson wouldn't like it."

He hesitated. She hoped he would remember that even Koss had to obey the captain. "I'll just be a minute." He put her down.

She changed into a midnight blue, high-necked, long-skirted dress. It wasn't easy changing in the closet, but she was grateful he didn't join her there. She was afraid he'd try to "help." But all he did was watch. She thought he seemed interested; but, at least he wasn't Pounder, and he didn't drool. If he hadn't been watching, she probably would have gone for her high-powered dart gun. She did insist on taking her purse. He didn't bother to search it, though her cosmetic bag would have passed any inspection.

On the way to the dining room, she mentally rehearsed various smiles and arguments. The halls and corridors were empty, and this puzzled her, although she'd already decided to not involve anyone else in a dispute with Ferenc—a dispute they'd surely lose.

When they got to the dining room, Koss and Pounder were on their way out. They looked worried. So was she. Where was Snark? She'd been relying on his presence to keep her safe. She stopped abruptly, coming up short against Ferenc. Her silvery blond hair flared out around her face and over her shoulders; she hadn't taken the time to put it up.

"There's trouble, Ferenc," Koss said, in a warning tone. "Stay close. Snark said the ship didn't feel right, and he's gone to check." Even as he spoke, Fissa was startled to see Ferenc's arm, not quite touching hers, shift subtly in color and texture. The golden brown skin took on a golden hue, almost metallic, and it somehow looked harder now.

She looked up to see Koss frowning at her. "We'll go to my rooms; there's equipment there we'll need. She goes with us."

Fissa didn't have time to protest; Ferenc took her firmly by the wrist. Though his grip was gentle, his skin was as hard as a rock.

They hadn't made it more than a few yards down the corridor when they heard the sound of running feet. Releasing Fissa, Ferenc leapt forward, crouching just before the corner. It was Snark, and he let him pass. Snark kept running. "Follow me," he gasped, and ran on into the dining room. The whole group broke into a tentative trot, but picked up the pace when they lost sight of him.

He stood waiting impatiently at the kitchen door. They followed him down two levels in the kitchen elevator, then down a dimly-lit passage way. As they hurried along, he explained, "We've been attacked. It's a much smaller ship, but quick and well armed... Probably a Combine ship, and it's now attached to us. That—and a surprise the captain's working on, should give us a chance to escape."

They stopped at an airlock. "I'm to take you off the ship," he announced, before turning to the airlock and activating it. He led them into a lifeboat, then went straight to the controls, where he inserted a program into the automatic pilot. They watched in silence as Snark worked at the control panel.

"Where are we going?" Koss suddenly demanded.

Snark made a final adjustment before turning away. "Snakebite," he said. "It's a nasty, unfriendly place, but it's close. There's a small relay—communications and minor ship repair—station there... It was a real bitch to establish, the captain said, but it'll slow down any pursuit, and, if anyone has a chance to make it, we do."

Koss nodded and said, "What are we waiting for?"

"The Captain's signal," Snark said. He glanced at Fissa. "Miss Skarvan needn't go with us. She'll only be in the way."

"Perhaps," Koss said, "but it's probably going to be a long, boring trip. She stays. And with her along, there's no doubt your captain will pick us up."

Snark hesitated only a second before turning back to the control panel, but it was long enough for Koss to say, "Put him out, Ferenc."

Ferenc grabbed Snark's wrist and twisted him away from the controls, hauling him roughly and inexorably to the door. "Don't hurt him!" Fissa screamed, just before Ferenc threw him out. Snark hit the passageway wall and slid slowly down it.

Koss had already turned away. "You're the pilot, Pounder," he said. "Take us out of here."

Fissa, having made a vain attempt to join Snark, had only bruises to show for it. In his armored mode, Ferenc made an effective barrier. "What about the captain's signal?" she asked sharply, resisting the urge to kick Ferenc.

"I think he lied about a signal. Anyway, we don't have much time," Koss said. "Sit down and strap in." Before he had finished the sentence, the lifeboat dropped away from the ship and accelerated.

Fissa made it to a rear seat and strapped herself in; Koss and Pounder sat at the control panel. Ferenc took the seat in front of her, placing himself between them. Probably not significant, Fissa thought, and although she doubted she had been any help to Snark, at least she'd tried.

Well, she'd wanted travel and adventure, and she was meeting new and interesting people. She was just sorry she didn't have her dart gun so she could have shot them. Still, she had those five make-up sticks in her cosmetic bag—three of them containing a gas-propelled disabling agent.

She could use the others to write messages. She also had tranq-powder, a pair of tweezers that could double as a small slingshot (to shoot bath pearls, which delivered a nasty sting followed by paralysis), and two extremely sharp nail files. The nail file case was actually a firing mechanism. Altogether, though, it didn't seem enough for this group.

She would have to get rid of Pounder and Koss first. She wished she understood better the relationship between Koss and Ferenc, but she was pretty sure that, with Koss out of the way, Ferenc would have no orders to follow. She'd decided, after meeting him, she wasn't going to start anything she couldn't finish.

"The auto program's taken over now." Pounder turned away from the controls and looked straight into Fissa's eyes. She stared right back. She had a makeup stick concealed in each fist; she knew they'd assume she was merely tense with fear. She would wait for them to come to her.

No way would these arrogant bastards suspect a thing. Watch it, you're getting twitchy, she warned herself.

Anyway, she had to wait, so that Ferenc wouldn't have the opportunity to interfere. The assumption was, Ferenc wasn't personally attached to Koss, and so wouldn't be into revenge. On the other hand, if she figured wrong...

The reality was, she actually was tense with fear. She had to make a conscious effort to relax her fingers, and not trigger the makeup sticks too soon.

"Ferenc," she softly whispered, anxious as Pounder came towards her. She'd unstrapped before arming herself. Now she leaned forward. She would have touched him if she didn't have her hands full. Still, she suspected he wouldn't feel anything in his current condition.

Suddenly Ferenc stiffened and stood up. I've done it, she thought with a great deal of pleasure, some pride, and a certain measure of relief. Pounder and Koss seemed more surprised than suspicious; but Ferenc merely stood, his head cocked to one side—and sniffed.

Freki. (She'd been taught to call on Woden's wolf when excited. Less vulgar, her mother said.) She was deeply disappointed and a little hurt. Curious, she stood up and deeply inhaled. Another mistake. It made her dizzy and disoriented. Bless you, Snark, was her last thought before she slipped to the floor at Ferenc's feet. Before losing consciousness completely, she saw Koss and Pounder fall heavily to the floor.

####

When Fissa awoke, she only missed losing consciousness again because Ferenc had snagged her by an ankle as she slid by him on her way to the control panel. With one arm wrapped around one of the two floor-to-ceiling supports in the middle of the lifeboat, he was also holding Koss, more or less upright, as the lifeboat plummeted straight down—presumably toward the planet. She twisted around, grabbing Ferenc's arm; he released her ankle and she managed to claw her way up.

Koss was barely conscious, hanging quietly in Ferenc's grasp. Fissa reached over and gently nudged him. "Where's Pounder?" she asked. "We have to do something—fast." From her vantage point, she couldn't see the pilot, and she was afraid to let go.

Koss shook himself and winced. "Broke something, I think," he said thickly, but he seemed more alert. "Good, he managed to strap himself in," he said, looking over his shoulder. "Put me in the seat next to him, Ferenc."

It was slow going, but Ferenc managed to get the three of them to the control panel without shaking Fissa off. Grateful, she did her best to stay out of his way as he maneuvered Koss into the seat next to Pounder. "Strap in," Koss told them impatiently as he concentrated on rousing Pounder.

At the sight of the pilot's head, Fissa became uneasy. The right side was dripping blood. And now she was sweating. The boat was hot, and getting hotter.

With a couple of stinging slaps and Koss screaming, "Wake up, you fool, we're going to die!" in his ear, Pounder rallied and managed to focus on the controls, wrestling with them until the boat finally leveled off. "I can't see," he murmured once. Koss took off his shirt, wiped Pounder's face with it, then wrapped it tightly around his head.

The boat slowly cooled off as Pounder fought the controls and struggled to stay conscious. The planet appeared on the overhead monitor, and Fissa couldn't take her eyes off it, as they slowed down and spiralled in. Koss ordered Pounder to look for the relay station, but after three fly-overs, they still hadn't spotted it, and Pounder couldn't get the radio to work.

Glancing down for a moment, Fissa saw blood seeping out of the sodden shirt. "We'd better land soon," she said, more concerned about Pounder than she'd ever thought she would be.

"Shut up," Koss snarled. "Remember what Snark said about this place."

Fissa realized, too late, that Koss couldn't see the bloodied side of the pilot's head. Before she could tell him, Pounder had slumped forward; the ship dived toward the planet's surface, hit, and somersaulted.

The seats broke loose on impact and Pounder and Koss flew forward. Ferenc and Fissa would have followed, but Ferenc grabbed Fissa and made his way back to the mid-structural supports by smashing his fist into the floor while dragging himself along.

Fissa found herself cradled against Ferenc's body, held tightly with one hand and arm protecting her head and neck, the other her back. He kept her away from the metal pole, bracing himself with his legs. That, and a prolonged series of crashes and bounces, was all she remembered.

###

She opened her eyes to blackness. She was lying on the floor—or ceiling for all she knew. She turned over cautiously. She felt bruised from head to toe, and her leg was cut and bleeding. Her skirt had apparently ridden up and she tried to pull it down. It was half gone; what remained was ragged edges and threads.

She reached out to feel around, but found nothing. If only she could find her purse; there was a torchlight in it. She'd lost the makeup sticks long ago; she wondered how long, as she kept feeling her way along the floor. One hand slid into a sticky pool—of what? Blood? It smelled like blood. Retreating, she dragged her hand across the floor to wipe it off.

She backed into a wall and crouched there, lost in the dark, with drying blood still on her hand; alone. "Ferenc," she whispered, suddenly afraid. She prayed it wasn't his blood. Kneeling, with both hands palms down on the floor so she could feel any vibrations in advance of sound, she listened.

Then the wall she was leaning against, began moving in and out, like breathing. A slow rending of metal followed, a squealing, stramash-like sound; and then there was light. She looked toward it. Ferenc was standing at the hole, enlarging it.

She stood, bracing herself against the wall. They'd landed right side up; the floor on her side of the ship was mostly level. The other side, near the side of the far support, was crumpled and bent, with a vee-shaped bend at the back. Its support was broken off at the bottom. The support on her side had buckled not more than a foot above where her (and Ferenc's) head had been. The ceiling above them was smashed in.

So far she hadn't seen...

Koss. He was crushed into the control panel by a pair of seats turned sideways. What was left of her skirt was caught on one of them, hung over the end and embedded in the control panel. All she could see was Koss' legs and workman-like boots, so incongruous with his formal suit. She looked away, drawing in a deep breath before beginning a search for Pounder.

She looked first for the blood; the congealed pool emerged from where the front right section of the control panel had folded in on itself. She didn't have to look any further.

Ferenc was still working. As soon as she got to him, he stopped. "That looks about right," she said, admiring the hole before looking out. "A bit high, though, isn't it?" The ground—bare gray sand, lay about five feet below them.

"The planet is dangerous, your friend said," he reminded her, in a tone of indifference. He leaned out to study something on the ground. The jagged metal edges didn't seem to bother him, Fissa noted. He must still be in his armored mode. Retreating, she began searching the ship for her purse and the two makeup sticks.

She found the purse wedged in a brace of seats, on the crumpled side of the boat. She was rummaging through it when Ferenc passed by and dropped a makeup stick in her lap. Then he began poking about in the storage compartments, breaking open the doors that had been sprung during the crash.

She joined him when he emerged from a mass of tangled metal. "Thanks for the makeup stick; I had two," she said, during a brief quiet spell. "But, look what I found in my purse. The communicator Mother gave me when I was still in school." She held it out to him. He took it, turned it over uncomprehendingly, and handed it back.

Fissa sighed. "I was afraid of that. I hope to use it to find the relay station." She took it to the window Ferenc had opened up and, sitting down in a square of light, she tried to get it working.

Finally, success. She gave thanks to her mother for her insistence on buying only the best. Then a shadow began waving back and forth over her head. "Snake!" she yelled and rolled towards the wall, fumbling in her purse for the makeup stick. She hit the trigger. There was a fizzling noise, followed by a feeble spit of liquid. That was enough, however, to trigger a response from the intruder. It pointed its long, yellow head at her. Quivering, it slid in further and dipped lower.

Then a golden hand grabbed it and pulled it in even more. Fissa scrambled to her feet, clutching the communicator, while wondering whether Ferenc was being prudent in his actions. She would have just tossed the creature out.

The snake whipped around Ferenc's arm and bit him. At least it tried. Gurgling, it decided to retreat, but Ferenc had already grabbed it with his other hand. Now he was pulling it apart. It soon split in two, flooding him with a pale, greenish liquid.

Fissa began moving towards him but backed off when he emphatically motioned her away. And for good reason: his clothes were sizzling where the liquid had splashed. She jumped back, checking the floor. "What should I do?" she asked, shocked to see his eyes were pale—almost opaque.

She looked around helplessly. Every time I think it can't get any worse, it does.

He was now stripping off his shirt, in bits and pieces. Fissa dipped into her purse again, looking for a scarf, the silver blue synthetic one she'd picked up at their last stop.

But when she turned back to Ferenc, he was already wiping his eyes with what was left of his shirt. She watched in fascination as a translucent membrane moved across his eyes, which soon returned to their usual orange color. Nor could she help noticing his chest; it was completely hairless and perfectly smooth. She wondered if it always looked like that.

Finished, Ferenc tossed the shirt out the hole. Fissa stared at him. There was a few holes on the outside of his pants, but it was the deep scars on his upper arms and back that held her attention. She'd heard of cultures that practiced ritual scarring. Was it punishment or rites of manhood, or could it have something to do with Koss?

She looked up to find him observing her in return. "Are you all right?" she asked hesitantly. He seemed especially interested in her legs.

"Yes," he said. With the help of a medical kit he'd unearthed, he cleaned and bandaged her leg. Then he returned to his relentless probing of the ship.

The acidic fluid had landed mainly on Ferenc, and what hadn't, dissipated, leaving rough splotches on the floor and walls. Fissa went back to working on the communicator.

Another shadow appeared, covering her completely. She yelped, throwing herself back; but it was only Ferenc. He hunkered down to see how she was doing.

"I'm almost done," she said with satisfaction. "This was really state of the art. It has all kinds of features, but the important thing is that it can talk to you." She frowned slightly. "I think another pass through the instructions and I'll get it right."

He looked at it. "It talks—to—you," he repeated slowly. Usually when he spoke, his voice was almost atonal, but this time, she thought she caught a hint of puzzlement.

She held it out to him. "When you press this button," she said, pointing to a green circle in the opened lid, "you activate it, and it tells you what to do. Just push it," she urged him.

"No. I cannot do such things easily NOW." He straightened up. Leaving her alone with the device, he continued ransacking the boat while she went back to the beginning, listening intently.

She found him squatting on his heels, sorting through what he'd accumulated. She knelt beside him, balancing the communicator on the palm of one hand, while pointing to the yellow dashes that crossed the miniature screen. "Where it's blinking is the direction we should go, I'm pretty sure."

"Yes," he said. "We start in the morning."

Fissa closed the communicator. "I suppose we can't just stay here and wait to be rescued?"

"To wait would be a mistake. Besides, there is no water. It is broken."

Usually his command of galactic was good—surprisingly so. She wondered what he meant by "broken water," but added, a little defensively, "Sometimes you're supposed to wait at the crash site."

He briefly looked at her, then turned back to his sorting. Amongst the battered, bedraggled collection, she spotted some clothing. Pulling the bundle toward her, she found overalls, shirts, socks, and even a pair of boots. Such foresight, she thought, until she realized that they were Koss'. She recognized the mud-brown workman's boots. She looked at his body, and saw his pathetic, naked feet—one of them bent at an unnatural angle. Shuddering, she turned back to Ferenc. "Thank you for the boots," she said.

"Yes," he replied, not looking up, his hands busy fashioning a pack out of a tattered blanket.

"I can carry a pack, too," she said coolly, and waited for his response.

"Yes," he said in his usual neutral tone. He dropped a food packet on top of the clothes piled in front of her, took one for himself, and went to the window to eat and watch.

Fissa found a pair of coveralls and shirt that fit and put them aside. She checked out the boots; they appeared to be clean and sturdy. She'd need no more than three pairs of socks to make them fit. Then she attacked the food packet. It wasn't a great meal, but she savored the fruit in its own juice.

Fissa spent the remaining hours before dark at Ferenc's side, studying the view from the window. She had plenty of time to observe the remains of the first inhabitant of Snakebite they'd met. It was a plant, with five broad, flat yellow-green leaves that tapered to a point at each end. Lying flaccid on the ground below, they were attached to a central stem that had terminated in an elongated, bell-like, pale yellow flower; now the stem lay in two rank and rotting pieces.

"What a stench," she said, when it was too dark to see. There was nothing more they could learn from their vantage point anyway. The plant's territory covered a circle at least twenty-five feet in diameter. Around it, stretching out in all directions, were identical plants. They'd have room to maneuver in the morning, if nothing else moved in. Which, she hoped, meant they'd have a quiet night.

In the darkness, Fissa furtively changed her clothes, took her purse and a blanket from Ferenc's pile of scavenging, and made a bed close to where he lay under the window. She felt safer there.

Lying on the blanket, on a hard, uneven floor, with a nasty gash on her leg, on a planet called Snakebite, did not prove conducive to sleep.

"Tell me about the broken water, Ferenc," she said.

"Busted in the crash. None left."

"Did Koss teach you to speak galactic?" she asked a little later.

"Yes. He had me taught."

She spent a few more minutes thinking how to phrase the question. "Where did you meet Koss?"

"Sleep now," he said firmly. Fissa wasn't sure, but she thought she'd detected a hint of reluctance in his voice. She turned over and tried to find a more comfortable position. No use...

In the morning, Ferenc roused her. He had changed into gray coveralls with no shirt. He wasted no time in getting started. As soon as she was awake and had pulled on her boots, they ate; then he dropped the pack out the window and immediately followed. Fissa slung her purse strap over her head, pushed the purse behind her back, and went to the hole.

Over the jagged edge Ferenc had hung a seat cushion ripped in half. He waited below while Fissa leaned against the cushion and looked at the ground. She remembered Koss' foot. "Jump," Ferenc said impatiently. He had given up hiding his emotions; she wondered how long it would take before he stopped saying "yes" to everything she said.

"Jump," he repeated, his orange eyes darker than usual—annoyance? He held up his arms and waited.

"Promise?" she said to herself, and jumped. He caught her and she clung frantically. She'd been afraid he wouldn't catch her; if he'd been an ordinary man, her fingers would now be digging deep into his flesh. When he put her down, she ruefully looked at her nails.

He put the pack on, with straps he'd salvaged from the wreck, and started off. It didn't take long to reach the edge of the dead plant's space. Ferenc discarded the pack and started forward.

Fissa hesitated. "Wait," she said. "You'll ruin your clothes again." She couldn't bring herself to advise him to take them off because they didn't have much in the way of replacements. "Isn't there a better way to do this, especially if we have to do it over and over?" The yellow blossom of the closest plant tilted toward them, stretching a little.

Keeping his eyes on the plant, Ferenc reconsidered. Then he made a fast approach. As it reached out to meet him, he leapt up, grabbed the blossom, pointed it away from his body, and tied the stem into a knot. It writhed and squirmed, trying to escape, but he continued—one knot after another—until the plant eventually quieted.

Fissa grabbed the pack and quickly shrugged into it. "Let's not waste time," she said. "I'll carry this for now."

"Yes."

They headed for the next plant, avoiding the leaves, which had never done more than tremble violently, much like ordinary leaves in a strong wind. But when Fissa looked back, the leaves were crawling to the stem. When she looked back again, she saw them probing the knot.

###

They camped that night inside the perimeter of another dead plant's territory. Ferenc twisted the stem off at the point when it was attached to the leaves, but he was still splattered with the acidic sap. "It's not so bad this time," Fissa said, after checking him out. He did lose most of one coverall strap. She even felt a little sorry for the plant.

After Ferenc wiped off the dried remains of the sap, they made camp between two of the long leaves. After laying a blanket on the ground and stretching out on it, they relaxed and cooled off a bit before opening their food packs. Snakebite was much warmer than Wodenhouse.

Fissa opened her packet, hoping to find something to drink. Not every pack had fruit in it, they'd learned. Fissa had found fruit in only one of her packets, though Ferenc had shared his with her. At three packets a day for two people, Fissa figured there was enough food for over a week. But how long could they go on with only a little fruit juice to drink?

Licking a drop of sweet juice off her lower lip, Fissa wished for water to wash it down. Ferenc had offered her some of his juice again, but she'd refused. Now she was lying there, waiting uncomfortably for dark. "It's probably a good thing there are just the two of us," she said, tentatively.

"Yes."

That, she thought, seemed heartfelt agreement. She continued. "Are you sorry Koss is dead?" No answer.

"He meant me harm, you know," she said with conviction. "I'm glad they're both dead. It isn't just the food packets."

"Yes."

Fissa sat up and stretched. She didn't want to go to sleep yet, but it wasn't long before she nodded off, waking up with a start when her head fell forward. Dark now, their only light source was a sort of phosphorescent glow from the dead leaves. She got up.

"What?" he said instantly.

"I'll be right back," she replied. She made her way gingerly over the leaves to the other side of the clearing, where she squatted. It wasn't any less embarrassing in the dark than it had been in the light of day, on the other side of a knotted plant. She envied him; he didn't really care.

The next day, the thirst and heat seemed worse. Then they came to the end of the plant life they had become accustomed to. They camped inside the circular territory of another dead plant, on the far side, away from the unknown, and stared at it.

This time Fissa didn't feel even faint regret for the plant Ferenc had to kill. Earlier that day they had come across one while it was feeding. The yellow blossom had attached itself to some kind of small animal. As it sucked vigorously, the leaves had swelled until they were no longer flat, and it continued to feed as they edged by.

"It looks like grass," Fissa said, "and mowed grass at that. I don't see anything living in it, not even weeds. It's just lush grass for miles most likely, with those burnt-looking trees here and there, but we can avoid them easily. What's the catch?"

"Yes," he said, and watched intently until dark.

The next morning, he made her wait while he strode off into the grass. Clutching the pack tightly, she sat there and watched, but nothing happened. He stopped some distance away but still within sight, and stood quietly for a few minutes before returning. Neither of them spoke. He then slipped on the pack, and they started off.

They were at least a mile into the thick, almost ankle-high grass before Fissa began to relax. Without thinking, she moved out from behind Ferenc to walk beside him; she was getting tired of seeing his back. Then her foot caught in something soft and sandy and she stumbled. A swarm of insects flew up in a buzzing fury and flurry of wings, covering her with stinging pricks of agony. She flung herself to the ground, curling into a ball for protection. Instantly, Ferenc picked her up, carrying her away from the nest.

As soon as they were free of the insects, he put her down. She sat, gritting her teeth, while he took off the pack and pulled out the medical kit. The insect bites itched and stung, and she felt nauseous. Ferenc applied a salve to all the bites, including those on her head, and removed a few small, black and green insects from her hair. Then he started going over the rest of her.

"How do you feel?" he asked, when she finally put a stop to his probing.

"Not too good, and I'm thirsty," she said. "I never saw a thing in that grass, though I did feel something—like a small, sandy mound."

"Wait here," he said. He headed back to the mound, treading deliberately around the area, arousing the nest again. He studied it thoroughly before heading off towards one of the trees in the distance.

Fissa slipped the purse strap over her head and dug through the contents of the bag until she'd reached the thick seam at the bottom. As soon as she felt the hidden opening by touch, she reset the anti-grav position up two notches. A lot of people had asked how she'd been able to carry so much in that purse. Custom-made, of course, even if it did seem too big to be elegant.

She hefted it up; she wanted to make it as light as possible. This trek was going to get tougher, and she didn't want to lose her purse or its contents; nor did she want Ferenc to have to carry it, if their situation became more difficult.

When Ferenc returned, she was in the process of securing her scarf tightly around her head. He was carrying a long branch from the tree. While tucking in the ends of her scarf, she considered it warily. "Did the tree give you much of a fight?"

"The tree was dead. Looks like the grass killed it."

Fissa, rising with alacrity, stared suspiciously down at the grass. "We probably should keep going, then." She gave a brisk brush to the seat of her dark blue coveralls.

Distrust of the grass was motivation enough to keep them moving steadily. They even ate standing up, although Fissa would have given a great deal just to sit and rest. The food packets at lunch each contained juice. When they had finished, Ferenc folded up the empty packets and returned them to his pack.

"You're certainly neat," she said, postponing what was really on her mind.

'It's wise not to leave a trail." He bent to pick up the pack.

She reached out and touched his arm. "Could I have some more juice?" she pleaded, looking at him with dark, desperate eyes. Her thirst had overcome her abhorrence of begging.

He considered her with his usual dispassionate gaze, then looked off into the distance. "How far do we have to go?"

"I'm not sure, but I am really thirsty." She didn't tell him she wasn't sure how much longer she could go on, with or without something to drink. What if she could no longer keep up? Would he abandon her? The thought was terrifying.

Now, as she searched his face for some sign of compassion, she didn't realize how much of her terror he could read; because, although he hadn't met that many beings off his home planet, other than Koss and his ilk, he had seen a lot of fear.

She stood there watching him, waiting, almost petrified with fear...hardly daring to hope. At last he reached out to her; she saw his hand change color, soften, as he ran his fingers over her face, letting them rest briefly on her forehead.

Saying nothing, he got out another food packet. No juice. Fissa, a sickly look on her face, stared at it, then Ferenc.

Without hesitating he pulled out another. This one contained juice and he handed it to her. "Eat the food, too," he commanded, wolfing his down and waiting for her to finish hers. As soon as she was done, he started off again, this time with Fissa walking several feet behind him as he probed with the branch.

That afternoon he flushed out two more nests, and, while he searched for a safe trail, Fissa rested. At their last stop, she had to force herself to get up. She staggered for the first few steps. She was hot, thirsty, and dizzy but straightened out for a few more steps before bumping into Ferenc's back. "We'll camp here," he told her.

As soon as he spread out the blanket, she collapsed on it. She awoke some time later, confused and groggy, to find Ferenc hauling her roughly to her feet. "The grass is attacking!"

Jerking the blanket up, he grabbed the pack and held her close to keep her from swaying. She clung to him, sick and scared. She wanted to vomit. It would serve the grass right, she thought bitterly. Nocturnal grass. That explains why it never bothered us before. Ferenc carried her a few more steps before suddenly stopping. It was too dark to see—no moon, a few dim stars, not even the phosphorescent glow from a decaying plant.

"Nests!" she suddenly remembered.

"Yes." He dropped to his knees, so that for a moment her back was touching the grass. She yelped, scrabbling to get free, but within seconds Ferenc too was lying on his back.

He rearranged the pack on his stomach and put her on top of it, wrapping her in the tightly-woven blanket, and held it all securely. There was no use trying to get comfortable. She couldn't move, and she was miserably hot, but eventually she fell into a light doze, only to be awakened when Ferenc began thrashing around.

"What's wrong?" she asked, hoping it wasn't the grass again.

"It's the grass," he said. After a minute of strenuously pounding the grass around them, he settled down again. At least twice that night, she awoke to Ferenc's battles with the grass. She had a vague feeling of having slept through one last, half-hearted attack.

But, in the morning, she was surprised to find herself actually feeling better, her thirst partially quenched by the juice she had for breakfast. She was so thirsty, the food didn't interest her at all, but Ferenc wouldn't budge until she'd finished it.

Before getting underway again, Fissa examined the grass. She felt a grim satisfaction in observing how flat it was lying in a circular pattern around them. "Did you get any sleep at all?" she demanded of Ferenc.

Shrugging, he shouldered the pack, picked up his stick and started off. How long can we go on like this? Fissa thought, dismayed. Even if we had water. Freki. She had told herself not to think about water—about cool, cleansing water.

As she trudged on, however, she found herself thinking not only about drinking, but about a long, soaking bath. With the scarf bound so tight, her head felt sticky, itchy and hot. But, at least it kept the insects out, otherwise they'd be trapped for sure in the salve-slimed mess that had now become her hair.

Then she ran smack into Ferenc's hard back and grabbed at him to keep from falling. "Is it time for lunch?" she croaked hopefully.

"No." There was a sharpness in his tone that startled her. He seemed to be studying something in the distance. Finally he moved purposefully around her and away. Frightened, she grabbed at his remaining coverall strap.

A mere fraction of a second later she was clutching tiny bits of cloth in her hand. The back of his coveralls were disintegrating! He turned back to her, a puzzled frown on his face. "The grass," she said to him in horror. "What will we do tonight?"

"Perhaps there will be no grass tonight." Pausing, he pointed. "Will you stay here and rest, or come with me?"

"I'm coming," she said without hesitation.

He started off, and she plodded along behind him. She could see his coveralls were shredded. He walked briskly, ceaselessly whipping the stick back and forth. And she followed, her mouth and throat parched and dry. Now she was fighting off not only thirst, but despair. He wanted to leave her behind; she was almost certain of that.

By focusing on his golden back, now clearly visible through the threadbare coveralls, she was able to stop herself before bumping into him when he finally stopped. "Yes," he said, with a hint of satisfaction and relief, as he pointed straight ahead.

She stared into the distance and saw what looked like a hill. Dark green, almost black, it rose gradually against the skyline. They made it to the rise as the setting sun, now at their backs, cast long shadows ahead of them. Fissa knew that meant they were no longer travelling in the right direction, but she didn't care.

A few feet from what appeared to be rock, Fissa stopped to let Ferenc check it out. He approached it slowly, going down on one knee to examine it closely. Fissa saw the color was green, but not the solid green it had appeared from a distance, rather shades of green running in swirls and streaks, shading into black here and there.

She sat in the grass and admired it; it was certainly the prettiest and most welcome thing she'd seen on the planet. When Ferenc slid down the rock face to land beside her, she asked, hoping, "No plants?"

This was the first time she'd seen him smile; the warm, contented feeling of security that washed over her made her temporarily forget her thirst.

But the climb up the incline, though gentle, brought it back with a vengeance. They stopped for the night at the first level space they found. Fissa pulled everything soft she could find out of the pack to make up a bed.

They had to go through four food packets before finding two with fruit juice. Again Ferenc offered to share his but she gritted her teeth and shook her head "no." Instead, she went to bed immediately, hoping they'd both get some much-needed rest. As they'd discovered, there wasn't much difference between the day and nighttime temperatures. Good, because she would much rather have the blanket under her than over her.

The next morning, only one packet contained juice and Ferenc made her drink it. "We can't waste any more of the food packets," he said. She knew opened food packets wouldn't keep, so she stopped arguing; her throat was parched and she was having difficulty swallowing. Besides, he was getting altogether too much practice at saying "no."

Before they started, Ferenc had her check the direction finder. "We can follow the rock for now," he said. They walked south, along the mostly level top of the ridge, which stretched ahead and behind them as far as the eye could see. Another rocky expanse stretched to the horizon on the east, while, to the west, the grass ran alongside.

They spent a quiet night on the rocky ridge, having stopped early when they'd found a slight hollow to bed down in—at least Fissa hoped it was for that reason, and not because she'd been stumbling more frequently.

As she fussed with her nest, Ferenc lay quietly on his back, staring up at the sky. They started early the next day. It was cooler, but she still didn't feel like getting up, especially since they had to endure a dry breakfast. The implacable Ferenc waited beside her, until she finally reached up, grabbed his arm and hauled herself up. She crumpled the food packet so he wouldn't see she hadn't eaten, though she suspected he knew. This time, however, he didn't insist she eat.

A few hours later, she was stumbling again. Concentrating was difficult, and she wasn't watching where she was going. Eventually he took charge, guiding and pushing her along with one hand on her shoulder. She vaguely hoped he wouldn't forget his own strength and accidentally crush it.

Then the rocky ridge began to break up under their feet. The solid rock gave way to narrow cracks and larger fissures, then bigger rocks with a scattering of smaller rocks and pebbles. Eventually the ridge tapered off, until they were surrounded by occasional boulders and myriad smaller stones; soon it was mostly uneven gravel, and treacherous to walk on.

At last Fissa stopped and refused to budge. Ferenc let go and she slowly sank to the ground. Now barely conscious, the desire to collapse became overwhelming. A few minutes later, she opened her eyes; he had made up her nest and slipped her inside. "Thank you," she mouthed. He was re-arranging some clothing under her head, and when his hand brushed the side of her face, she kissed it, then went to sleep.

She awoke to find the sun only a few hours from setting, and Ferenc lying on his stomach beside her, his arms folded against his chest, and studying her. "Sorry," she mouthed while struggling to get up.

She turned over, got one knee under her, and paused to catch her breath. He made her lie down again. "I can give you water," he said softly. "Do you wish it?"

"Yes," she said, forcing out the word.

He leaned over, cradling her head in his hands. Her eyes fixed upon him, with hope and wonder, as she saw his skin lose its golden glint; she felt his fingertips, soft upon her face. He bent his head; his lips touched hers and clung, and his mouth, touching hers, opened. With a sudden shiver of trepidation, she responded by opening hers.

Almost as soon as their lips were sealed, she felt her mouth fill with water, oddly warm but welcome. She closed her eyes and swallowed. She felt its flow—refreshing, renewing, relaxing. She also felt a dreamy contentment.

When she opened her eyes again, it was nearly dark. Ferenc lay beside her on his back, arms folded under his head. His skin was still golden-brown and soft, and she wondered briefly if the gravel bothered him. She turned over and faced him. "Thank you," she murmured.

His eyes, dark orange—darker than she remembered ever seeing them, were watchful. He seemed a little tense. She rested her head on his chest for a few minutes, savoring the relief she felt—in body and mind—until he shifted position and put his arms around her, gathering her even closer.

Fissa stiffened and pushed away. His arms held her, rock-hard, tightening more. She arched her back and snarled. Pushed. To no avail. She tried to back out from under his arms. Just when her mind went into attack mode—nails, teeth, and purse—he released her.

Troubled, she backed away to the perceived safety of her nest, studying him as he returned to his former position on his back, arms folded under his head. For a while she eyed him suspiciously, but soon the feeling of contentment—and closeness—returned.

Again she approached him; this time he remained still as she rested lightly on his chest, studying his face. His eyes were deep, widely-set, with heavy solid-looking lids covering them. His nose was broad, and solid-looking, too, but the naris was small. Of course, she thought, it would be easier to protect that way.

Her fingers followed her gaze, down to his lips—thin and a little rough to the touch—obviously another safety feature. Her examination shifted to his hair; touching it, she found the rich brown strands coarser than they looked. She wondered what happened when he went into his armored mode. That would be interesting to see—and touch. She enjoyed touching him. From the first time they'd met, she'd found him fascinating; but now? She lowered her head and kissed his lips.

This time he moved slowly and gently, and she found herself revelling in the touch of his hands upon her skin. Eventually the tentative questing gave way to an evermore demanding touch, and she responded eagerly. He removed her clothing in an unhurried fashion, careful not to startle her, even as she snuggled and nuzzled him. Though she hardly noticed, he never stopped studying her face.

She knew only the desire to be close to him, the pleasure of his gentle touch. Then he suddenly wrapped himself around her. There was an instant of awareness, where she issued a muffled, but somehow essential, "I love you." Then consciousness blurred into passion, followed by such merged mutual delight, it left them clinging together for some time afterward. She nestled against him for a while before finally falling asleep.

The next morning, she awoke curled up cozily with Ferenc in her nest. For a confused moment she stared at her hand, which was now resting on his chest, and thought: His coveralls have totally disintegrated. Then she remembered.

Smothering an anguished gasp, she tried to think. It hadn't been rape because she'd been willing. She squirmed, remembering just how willing she'd been. It must have been something in the water. Had he intended...?

Confused and apprehensive, she lay frozen, afraid to stir, afraid to wake him, trying to get her thoughts and feelings in order. He isn't like the others, she told herself. Then she recalled what she'd managed to do—to say—despite being engulfed in an emotional maelstrom: "I love you."

Well, of course... that made it all right. Sure. But in reality, the words were nothing more than an excuse for lack of control—or so her mother always said, and she agreed. She bit off a strangled moan. *But enough about me. What about him? How does he feel? That's what's most important now—how does he feel about me?*

And then he was leaning over her. She stared at his golden body, in fascination, remembering, before forcing herself to look into his eyes. She knew instantly what he wanted and bared her teeth. He tensed but continued his approach, reaching for her. She snarled. He stopped, considered, then withdrew.

Fissa turned over, searching desperately for her clothes. She was lying on them. He'd probably done that. She knew she should be grateful, but she was feeling too embarrassed, resentful, confused.

She threw on her clothes, keeping her back to him even after she was dressed. Though no longer thirsty, she was ravenous, and searched through the pack, pulling out two food packets. There were only five left. Dismayed, she braced herself and turned to tell Ferenc.

To her relief, he had put on a pair of green coveralls. She searched the ground nearby and soon spotted a pile of grayish cloth and ash. "Wow!" she said, blushing. "I mean..." She pointed to the pile. "Are you all right?"

He looked at her impassively; then his eyes softened into a lambent orange flame. A flame she had seen and felt, and now found herself responding to again. Strange she only remembered it now. Disturbed by her reaction, she stepped back, skidded, and went down, hands and knees on the gravel. The sharp, painful jolt brought her quickly to her senses.

He was going to help her up, but she scrambled away from him. "I see we're low on food," she said, looking down at the pack. "It's my fault." She brushed some grit off her palms. There was gravel embedded in her hands, and blood where she'd scraped and torn the flesh, in her haste to get away from him.

Ferenc, glancing at her hands, dug out the medical kit. After a brief resistance, she let him clean her hands, relaxing against him as he ministered to her needs, studying his face as he worked. Soon she was nuzzling his face.

This time, he pushed her away. "Not now," he said with some reluctance in his voice. He was admonishing himself as well; she could see the resoluteness of his expression. It was a tangible thing and she was tempted to test it, as a fledgling tests its wings. You've always scorned women who indulged in such tricks, she reminded herself. She picked up the food packet.

They ate quickly. Ferenc's packet had fruit and juice, but when he glanced her way, she refused it. She finished first and took advantage of the shelter of a nearby rock. When she returned, Ferenc slipped on the pack, picked up his stick, and they resumed their journey.

They made good time that day, stopping only once to rest; it helped that the gravel had given way to broken rock. It was mostly level. Fissa had no trouble keeping up, and she was no longer worried about being left behind.

Late that afternoon, Ferenc stopped, head up, to sniff the air. She remembered how he'd been the first one to smell the sleeping gas in the life boat, and she sniffed the air, too. But all she could smell was the stale, sweaty odor of her own, unwashed body. Apparently, he didn't sweat—probably another defense mechanism, which might explain why he had water to spare.

She followed close behind as he angled off, and a little further on she caught the scent—water. Before long, they were on solid rock again; ahead and slightly below them was a pool, apparently carved out of the rock. There were several boulders, oddly squared, nearby, as if carelessly tossed there by whatever had dug out the pool.

Fissa considered the pool, and was shocked to realize how grateful she was they hadn't found it sooner. But now she could have a bath and wash her hair. She wondered if they were going to have to chip the scarf loose.

As she started toward it, Ferenc stopped her, with a firm—just short of crushing—grip on her shoulder. "It doesn't look friendly," he warned.

Fissa took a closer look: The pool was in shadow, the water murky; but she had attributed that to the boulders shading it in the lowering sun. Stepping back, she watched uneasily as Ferenc dropped the pack at her feet and slowly approached the pool.

As soon as he dipped the long branch into the water and began to probe, the end of the stick took a sudden dive. Something was tugging on it. Ferenc, tightening his grip, whipped the stick sideways out of the water, away from him. Several elongated white blobs splashed upon the rocks around the pool, oozing and surging shapelessly, then slipped back into the pool with hardly a ripple.

Fissa clutched her purse. "Leeches!" she said, reaching inside for the cosmetic bag.

"Leeches?" he asked, as they both stepped back.

"Bloodsuckers," she explained.

"Yes," he said. "I wonder if the whole planet is infested."

She shivered. Thank God we didn't find the pool when I was thirsty.

They didn't linger. Pushing forward steadily, they didn't slow down until the rocky ridge began to break up again. It was almost dark when they stopped. The broken pieces of rock were sometimes separated by fissures they had to jump across.

They bedded down on what was really a narrow ledge, being a foot or more higher than the rest of the rock. Fissa felt safer on the ledge, but it was so narrow they couldn't sleep side by side; she was ambivalent about that. Ferenc gave her the blanket and the extra clothes from the pack to lie on.

Fissa slept fitfully, worried about falling off, and once she woke up trembling. "Leeches," she said under her breath, and looked around uneasily. It had been a remarkably vivid dream. She reached out to touch the hard, dry rock, and reassured, drifted off to sleep once more.

The next morning she woke stiff, hungry, and thirsty. Stretching gingerly, she turned over to see Ferenc climbing up to the ledge. He gathered up the pack and contents and led the way down to a level space where they ate their breakfast. Both packets had juice; Fissa was relieved.

After the meal she checked her direction finder. Although it seemed the flashes were closer together than before, she wasn't sure if that meant they were actually getting closer to the station. She switched over to the instruction setting, to eliminate the possibility of a power problem.

"According to this," she said, "we're almost there."

"Good," he said, crushing the food packet he was holding even smaller than usual.

"Well, we're almost out of food, and probably everything on this planet is more likely to hunt us than to let us hunt them. And I need a bath." That, at least, was a more cheerful thought, and she got up.

The ridge continued in the right direction, sometimes solid and sometimes slightly cracked, for several miles. Fissa was sure it was several miles anyway, as she felt her mouth and throat get drier and drier, an all too-familiar feeling. When the ridge made a sudden turn to the east, she was grateful for the chance to stop and rest while they considered the situation.

Their goal lay straight to the south, through plants—bushes this time—that grew closer together than the large flowering plants they'd left behind. The bushes were a dull gray-green, with a multitude of spiny stems, sticking out of the gray sand at almost 45o angles, in a thickly-bunched circle.

"Not friendly, I bet," Fissa said.

"No," he agreed, "but beyond them..."

She stared in the direction he indicated, but could see nothing. She rummaged hopefully in her purse. "Next time," she said, "I'll remember to pack my distance glasses; they're back on the ship. I could even carry a flask. It's a good thing..." She broke off abruptly.

He glanced at her purse, but said nothing. She had a feeling he was no longer surprised whenever she came up with something new from deep inside it.

"I think it's the station. I see a dome," he said. "We'll cross in the morning." But, instead of making their usual simple camp, he set off along the ridge. Puzzled, she followed. She was feeling increasingly baffled and thirsty when at last he stopped. He'd found a large hollow in the rock with an overhang from a ledge above. It was almost a cave.

"We camp here," he said, spreading the blanket carefully and smoothly over the remaining clothes from the pack. Fissa stared uneasily at the inviting nest; she wasn't surprised when he asked, "Are you thirsty?" She was thirsty. She'd been trying to put it out of her mind, postpone the decision she'd have to make, forewarned with the knowledge she hadn't had the first time.

If she said yes, this time she wouldn't have the excuse of ignorance. She lay down, and he dropped beside her, but was careful not to touch her. She closed her eyes and tried to think. When she finally opened her eyes—to just a slit—peeking out beneath her lashes, he was looking down at her quietly and calmly, but she could see that the fire was merely banked. He was either being considerate or wary.

She shut her eyes again. She thought about her mother, the standards she had been taught and still believed in, what people would think, and more important, what Snark and the crew would do to Ferenc if they knew; and she looked at and rejected the argument that, after all, it didn't matter now because she'd already given in once.

She couldn't use the excuse of thirst because she'd been in worse shape and survived. Anyway they were nearly there; after that... No matter what happened between them, she had to think about afterwards. "I love you," she'd said, activating her own defense mechanism. Did she mean it? What about him?

She looked at him again. He was patiently watching her—his eyes darkly orange, the skin golden brown. She admired his strength and his control, but—he was so very unlike anyone she'd ever known in her world—physically and otherwise—and, despite his strength, he would be very vulnerable in that world when they were rescued.

Fissa remembered Captain Saknusson with a jolt. She might have to deal with a man almost as dangerous as Ferenc. He probably wouldn't hesitate to kill Ferenc if he even thought...

She looked worriedly at Ferenc and saw that worry reflected in his eyes, though his was not of the future. Softening, she felt an unexpected compassion and affection, for the first time actually caring about what he thought. She brushed her fingers along his cheek and said, "Yes." She meant to add, "I'm thirsty," but his lips were already on hers.

She drank the warm, welcome water, felt again that feeling of complete relaxation and contentment. This time he, too, waited until she roused from the lassitude that overcame her. She puzzled over it briefly, wondering what it would be like without the giving of water. Then he touched her.

She responded with an intensity and eagerness she hadn't felt before. This time, she was more aware of what was happening, so that later, as they relaxed side by side, she was able bring herself to ask about something that puzzled her.

"I noticed..." she said tentatively, " that you avoid touching..." She gritted her teeth and went on, "my breasts. Most women like to be touched there." I've come a long way, she thought, from not knowing what I was doing, to telling him what I want him to do.

Silence. She had given up expecting an answer, when he suddenly turned over and said, "I know. I have seen it on Koss' tapes. I learned much..."

"Is it taboo, then?" she finally asked. "That is—a forbidden thing?"

"Yes."

"Do your women have breasts?" she asked, struck by an incredible thought.

"Not like yours." He said it regretfully, she thought.

"How do...? That is, what about your babies—your young, I mean?"

He withdrew for a long time, seeing something she couldn't imagine. "Our young suckle as yours do," he said with deliberateness, "but for men, it is forbidden."

"I'm sorry," she said, appalled. "I want..." she said. And stopped. Did she have the right to want him—to urge him—to break such an ingrained taboo?

She wouldn't ask him. Instead... "Perhaps we should go on," she suggested, moving as if to get up. His response was instantaneous. This time there was hardly a square inch of her body that his hands and mouth didn't explore. Her response was no less ardent than his, though once she had to fight off that curious lethargy she'd experienced before, which was strange. Was it to give him time to escape?

They spent that day and night in their nest, alternating between sleeping and not, though as time passed, he watched her ever more carefully before making his approach. The next day they slept late, so that by midday, Fissa was ravenous. After eating, she pulled the last food packet out of the pack. "We'd better save it for tomorrow," she said.

"We should go on," Ferenc said, with a hint of reluctance.

Fissa was even more reluctant. She was fairly certain she had spent more time considering the consequences than he had. "Perhaps we should wait till tomorrow," she said. "It's late, and we want to be sure we reach the dome before dark. I'd hate to spend the night among those bushes."

"Yes." He gave her one of his rare smiles and reached for her. She wondered briefly if smiles were also taboo in his culture. And she should learn more about the sharing of water and its aftereffects ...

The next morning, Fissa was the first to awake. It was still dark, but there wasn't much time left. She woke him up and they held each other close, their passion tinged with foreboding, until she pulled unwillingly away. After they ate, she watched in silence as he folded up the food packet into an incredibly small piece of plastic, returned everything to the pack, and got up. She searched his face; she would have welcomed the tiniest trace of a smile, but he was even more impassive than usual—grim, in fact. He glanced at her, then turned away and started off. She followed.

They retraced their steps to where the ridge had come to an abrupt bend. Descending cautiously down the uneven and pebbled slope, Fissa stopped at the bottom and waited, leaning against a solid block of marbled green and black rock.

Ferenc strode steadily to the nearest bush. It looked more gray than green today, and the tiny spines on its rigid stem-like trunks were rustling softly, though there wasn't a breeze to be felt. Ferenc wrapped both arms around the bush and heaved. As he did, the bush tried to wrap itself around him, but there wasn't time, nor could its spines penetrate his flesh. In one smooth motion, he pulled it out of the ground and heaved it on top of its nearest neighbor.

What looked like a wrestling match between the two bushes ensued. It wasn't long before the bush on the bottom got the upper hand over its drop-in guest, and the first bush's remains—small sticks—littered the ground around it.

Gradually the winning bush quieted until its rustling died down to a soft sigh. Ferenc considered it for a minute before heading for the next bush in line. That bush made a valiant attempt to fight back, but it too was tossed onto a nearby bush. This time the host bush merely gave the other bush a vigorous shake and tossed it away.

The uprooted bush started to crawl back to its hole, but Ferenc just stood there, watching. The bush huddled close to the ground and shivered. Ferenc studied it uncertainly. Then he made a tentative move towards it. It shrunk closer to the ground. If it could have whimpered, Fissa thought, it would have.

She stepped away from the rock ridge and moved a few feet closer to Ferenc, but he motioned her back and headed for a different bush. This bush, bigger than those around it, clattered its spines angrily as if to challenge him. Ferenc went to it eagerly. You picked the wrong day, thought Fissa, to mess with this man.

Ferenc gathered the big bush in a crushing grip and then twisted it apart, tossing each half on top of a different bush. The two halves were thrown aside violently, and every bush within Fissa's view quivered. The next bush Ferenc approached leaned as far away from him as it could, until it was almost touching the ground, a few roots on the side closest to Ferenc pulling out of the sand.

Fissa, hesitating no longer, went to join Ferenc. He let her approach, alert to any hostile movement from the bushes, but none stirred. He led them through, with Fissa close behind, while every bush they approached prostrated itself before them.

Thanks to the bushes' capitulation, they made excellent time. They paused twice to rest, while all the nearby bushes lay quietly in a large circle, pointing away from them. By the second stop, Fissa could see the dome.

Since leaving the ridge, neither Ferenc nor Fissa had said a word. They were careful not to disturb the truce with the plants; Ferenc had nothing to say, and Fissa was aware that the closer they got to the dome, the more chance there was of anything they said being picked up.

It was mid-afternoon when they left the bushes' territory behind. Between them and the massive dome lay a vast expanse of black, crystallized sand. Fissa picked up a dark, glittering handful and let it drift back to the ground through her fingers. "Could be a force-field or a periodic burn; better wait here," she said.

When nothing happened in a half an hour, Fissa threw a handful of the black sand against the side of the dome. Then she asked for admittance, starting with a quiet, reasonable request, more sand, finally ending up with annoyed yells and an occasional full-throated shriek. "It makes me feel better," she told Ferenc after the first time, when he had leaped to his feet in a instinctive reaction.

The last incredibly shrill, drawn-out shriek had almost done her in, leaving her hoarse and thirsty. As she pondered her next move, they heard the approaching crunch of feet on the sand. Fissa pulled out her cosmetic case and palmed a makeup stick; then, slipping the case into a coverall pocket, she stood beside Ferenc to wait.

The first thing she noticed was the large, drawn and leveled weapon. Then she recognized the figure. "Snark! Am I glad to see you." She stepped in front of Ferenc. Although she didn't really expect him to stay put, she was still annoyed when he pushed her aside.

"The gun isn't necessary, Snark," she said, thinking he had be stupid to think of threatening Ferenc with it; but her icy glare probably gave him a hint of her feelings.

Shrugging, Snark holstered the gun. Looking around, he asked, "Is it just the two of you then?"

Nice recovery, thought Fissa. "Yes. Koss and Pounder are dead—killed in the crash. With Ferenc's help I'm still alive."

"I'm glad," Snark said. He led them almost half way around the huge dome to the entrance. In front of the dome, a landing field of the same black sand stretched out to the south; it was big enough for several ships, though only two small shuttles were parked there.

Snark said nothing more until they'd passed through the oversize double doors and were safely inside. Fissa noticed that the inside door didn't open until the outer one had closed.

"What took you so long?" Snark asked in a conversational tone, just barely including Ferenc in his sideways glance. Fissa glared at him as he crossed to a monstrous console, behind which they could see only the top of a man's head.

Circling the console, they saw that it wasn't that the man was short; rather the console was tall—and wide. Floor to ceiling columns ran in two long lines to the back wall. Another airlock was inside the two lines, along with a crowded assortment of furnishings. "Very impressive," Fissa said, smiling at the tall, wire-thin man sporting a high rise hairdo (black with pale blue accents), which was the only reason they'd seen the top of his head.

"Benjamin Franklin Fuller, I'd like you to meet Anfissa Skarvan and her companion-in-peril on this planet, Ferenc." With an engaging grin, Snark surprisingly included Ferenc in his introduction.

"Call me Benfry," Fuller said, stepping forward to shake their hands. Apologetically, Fissa extended a grimy hand.

"We were short of water on our trek," she explained. "I have been looking forward to a bath for a long time."

"We're a bit short on water here ourselves," Fuller replied, apologizing in turn, "but for you we'll make an exception." He turned toward Ferenc, his hand extended, but Ferenc made no move to take it. Instead, he radiated an unmistakable air of hostility.

"They don't shake hands in his culture, I believe," Fissa said.

"More likely to take them off at the wrist," Snark added. "Speaking of which, shouldn't Rodriguez be back already?"

Fuller prudently stepped away from Ferenc. Now he sat down in a tracked chair in front of the console's control panel. "The tank's secure, but slow," he said. "I'll check."

A curious Fissa joined him at the curved control console. It had been impressive enough on the other side, but here was an array of switches, buttons, and dials that made those in the lifeboat look like a video game. "Come in, Manny, come in," Fuller called after flipping a switch. "All secure, and we have the visitors we've been hoping for." There was a scratchy reply.

"He said he'll be right in," Fuller told them. "I don't open the door though till I get his signal." A half minute later they heard a full-bodied honk which resounded throughout the great room. Fuller laughed at their expressions. "Sorry. It's hard to regulate transmission because of the denseness of the dome. That's why we couldn't hear you. There're no outside pickups."

"But how..?" Fissa began, interrupted as Fuller activated the outer and then the inner doors. What looked like a big metal box, trundled in on head-high and immense treads.

Manny Rodriguez, as short as Fuller was tall, was even friendlier. There were just the two of them stationed here, responsible for spare parts and repair robots; they were always ready for visitors, one way or another.

Actually we haven't had any intruders since the first two tries right after the dome was finished, but we don't take chances, especially since the outside sensors don't last long. The only reason we're here is that we don't have to import air, just filter it."

"So why did you come looking for us?" Fissa asked.

"My shuttle picked up your screaming and contacted me," Snark said. "I've been here for a few days, hoping you'd turn up, and waiting for equipment. Your mother had heavy gear shipped immediately, but even she couldn't get it delivered any sooner than next week. I'm glad you two made it." Again Snark included Ferenc—this time with a heartfelt smile, but he refrained from slapping him on the back.

"I wouldn't have without Ferenc." Fissa never missed a chance to give him the credit.

"But how did you do it?" asked a curious and still incredulous Fuller. Fissa hesitated. She'd observed that Snark had avoided mentioning Ferenc's special abilities. She decided to do the same.

"We came down hard," she said. "It wasn't just a crash, but a lot of crashes—the way I remember it. We woke up almost too late to land. By the way, Snark, thanks for the tranquilizer. That was your doing, wasn't it?"

"Yes," he said, a little puzzled, "but you should have had plenty of time to prepare for a landing."

Fissa examined the remains of her nails thoughtfully. "That may have been my fault," she said. "When the gas hit, I was holding two gas producers of my own. The one I found afterwards was empty." All the men, including Ferenc, nodded in understanding. Considering all she'd survived, somehow they weren't in the least bit surprised.

"Koss and Pounder were killed in the crash; it was messy," she said, dispensing with the details. "We made it through assorted plants—not your friendly lily types—until we were lucky enough to come across a wide area of rock. It was easier then. Water was a problem," she paused for a second, "but we managed. We even found a pool, but it was full of more nasty planet life."

"Great midnight skies of Jamac!" said Rodriguez "I've heard of that pool. Three planet surveyors camped there. During the night they heard some scratching noises on their portahut; two of them went out to check, with lights and guns. The other one was still half-asleep; he was pulling on his pants when they started screaming. 'Lock the hut, lock the hut,' one had the sense—and the guts—to yell. He did; whatever it was couldn't get in."

Fissa was still trying to unclench her hands when Snark broke the silence. "What happened?"

"The two men were gone without a trace. The survivor refused to stay on the project. 'I hope the screaming will stop if I get off the planet," he said. They gave him extra pay, I believe."

"That's why we're here," Fuller said. "Extra pay, a year's tour of duty, and a step up in grade."

"You've earned it," Snark said with respect. He looked at Fissa. "I take it you weren't there at night."

She shook her head violently. "We saw them though—rotten little leeches, like most everything else on this planet."

"You were lucky," Fuller said. "You crashed in the experimental plots."

In a single flowing movement, Fissa got to her feet. "Those are your experiments?!" she said, staring at him hard.

Fuller moved away in sudden alarm. "No, no," he hastened to assure her. "Someone or some thing planted those plots and put up that rock wall around them. The rest of the planet is a jungle. There, you have not only plants, but animals, to contend with. Like I said, you were damn lucky."

"That was a wall?" Fissa asked, sitting down again..

"Yes," Fuller said. "It's old and breaking down, but still doing a pretty good job of keeping the animals out."

"We only saw one animal," Fissa said. "The plants got it."

"The animals are even nastier than the plants and quicker, of course. That's why we put the dome inside the wall. Even so, those first two tries were hairy—in more ways than one. You see the pillars; plastisteel shutters make a cocoon around them, if we can make it to the console in time."

Fissa looked at the two men with open admiration. "I think I've spent all the time on Snakebite I want to." Turning to Snark, she demanded, "How soon do we go? And what happened on the St. Catherine?"

Snark pulled back his lips, showing his teeth in a snarly smile. "Well, I was unconscious for a while so I missed some of the fun. But Captain Saknusson took advantage of the fact that our attackers had attached themselves to us. He shoved something hot up their tail, then used our repellors to kick them loose. We managed to get far enough away, so when their ship blew, we suffered only minor dents."

"That was quick and easy," Fissa said. "We could have stayed..." She bit her tongue when she saw the slight stiffening of Ferenc's body, but apparently no one else noticed.

Snark shook his head. "There were fourteen men still aboard," he said in reproach. "There was some vicious infighting. The captain enjoyed it, naturally. You know about his hunting trips, I imagine."

"What hunting trips?" she asked. Mother had told her very little about her cousin.

Snark, suddenly ill at ease, shrugged. "They're dangerous, that's all," he said. "He says most animals offer no challenge to a real hunter..."

"He hasn't been to Snakebite, then," Fissa said drily.

"I'll have to tell him about this place. No doubt he will want to talk to you about your visit," Snark said in retort. "Anyway, I got in on the tail end of the fighting. I guess I wasn't quite up to it yet. Captain Saknusson had to slice off a man's hand. The guy had a bead on me, but I never even saw him," he said in disgust. "That's pretty much it."

"Did the hand end up on the captain's trophy wall?" Fissa wondered aloud.

Snark shot her a startled look. "Could be," he said. He stood up, pushing his chair under the table. With most of the furnishings inside the lines of pillars, there wasn't much room. "We can take off any time," he added.

"They just got here," Fuller protested, "and she hasn't had her bath yet." He flushed. "Nor eaten."

"Too true," said Fissa. She'd forgotten about the bath. Now she wondered how obvious her need was. And she was starving.

"I know you have to ration your water," Snark replied. "They have to haul it in," he explained to Fissa. "You can wait until we reach the ship. She's in orbit."

"Here?!" Fissa exclaimed. "I thought they'd dropped you off..."

"People were worried about you; apparently your mother can really put on the pressure." Snark gave her a thoughtful stare.

Trying not to blush, Fissa looked back at him coolly. She'd need all the practice she could get, after all.

Fissa could see that Fuller and Rodriguez were disappointed; they'd been willing to sacrifice precious water so she and the others would stay a little longer. Now, as Fissa, Ferenc, and Snark headed out to the shuttle, the two men went so far as to wave good-bye from outside the outer doors.

Before entering the shuttle Fissa stopped for a last look around. "It seems so peaceful," she said. "It's hard to believe how close you usually are to new and nasty ways of dying." She had half-expected to be pursued across the field as the planet's way of bidding them farewell.

"Fortunately, a lot of the native life seems most aggressive at night," Ferenc said, surprising them both.

Snark was ready to encourage him. "I wonder how much of it is nocturnal. I didn't see anything of the plants or animals here except on tapes at the station."

"Perhaps you two can do a study on it sometime," Fissa said as she entered the shuttle. Snark grinned at Ferenc, but didn't seem surprised to see the shuttered look back on his face. He dogged the door shut and headed forward.

Fissa recognized the two crewman who'd been left on the shuttle—Sam Walsh and Eric Falcone—and greeted them with just a hint of a smile. She was growing increasingly nervous as she faced the inevitable confrontation with the captain; and she was certain her mother would turn up soon.

Walsh, the pilot, was short, dark, and quiet. He merely said, "Welcome back," and set about getting ready for lift-off. Falcone, red-headed and curious, was bubbling over with questions, but Snark stopped him. "Later," he said.

Fissa appreciated being left alone. She curled up on a row of seats on one side of the shuttle. Ferenc sat down a little farther back on the opposite side. Snark was up front with the two crewmen; she could hear him talking on the radio, but couldn't hear what he was saying.

An hour later the shuttle had homed in on the St. Catherine and berthed. Too soon, thought Fissa, more than a little apprehensive when Snark told her to report to the captain. "I am not going anywhere except to my quarters for a bath,'" she said flatly. He nodded in understanding.

###

At least an hour for a bath, she thought, as she lay soaking in water kept hot automatically. While most of the passengers and crew had to make do with sonic showers, her suite came with water rights. She was still in the tub when her comm chimed. "The captain's compliments, and he expects you to be in his office in fifteen minutes."

It could be worse, she told herself while dressing. It could've been my mother. She can read me like a booktape. She arrived two minutes before the deadline. Captain Saknusson stood when she entered his office, and waited while she took a seat. "I'm eager to hear about your adventures on Snakebite," he said affably. He settled back, rock solid, in a winged chair upholstered in an unfamiliar, mottled brown leather, his green eyes fixed steadily on her face.

Fissa gave him a fairly faithful, glowing account of how Ferenc had brought her, unscathed, to safety, dwelling on the malevolent planet life, while avoiding the personal details. At the end she thanked him for sending Snark and waiting for her.

"Even if your mother hadn't been so insistent," he informed her with a wide, warm smile that completely changed and softened his face, "I would have done so."

"Mother..?" said Fissa slowly. "Where is she? I suppose she's going to meet the ship at our next stop?"

The captain's smile broadened as he shook his head. "No. I told her not to. I said you were adult enough now not to be coddled or escorted home like a wayward child. I believe she is waiting for you on Wodenhouse."

Impressed, Fissa stared at him. "However did you manage that?" She could hardly believe it.

His red-blond mustache, not quite as red as the thick-growing thatch on his head, twitched. "She trusts my judgement," he said with open amusement. Then the affability, which had lulled Fissa into a false sense of security, switched off. "Tell me about Ferenc," he commanded, and if there was such a thing as green steel, his eyes were made of it.

Taken aback, Fissa's throat felt suddenly dry, reminding her vividly of the planet she'd recently left. "I told you," she began.

"Tell me about him. Did you feel safe with him? Was there any time you thought you couldn't trust him?"

"No," she said defiantly, and immediately knew she'd made a mistake. Flushed with annoyance and self-reproach, she continued, "The only time I didn't feel safe," she insisted, "was before we crashed. After Koss and Pounder were dead, I didn't worry—well, not very often."

"Did he tell you anything about himself?" he asked.

She looked at him warily. "He told me Koss had him taught Galactic; I don't know any more than that." She leaned forward and tried not to sound too anxious. "What's going to happen to him?"

"He's from an interdicted planet. Usually that means he must be returned. However..." He pinned her with his steel-green gaze. "...did you happen to notice his scars?"

She blushed again, grateful for the tan she'd picked up on Snakebite. Perhaps it would make the blush less obvious. "He got some acid on him once from the big plants—I told you about that. It wreaked havoc with his clothes." She wished she could stop blushing, but she did manage to keep her chin up and look him straight in the eye.

The captain steepled his long, thick fingers. "The culture is a very inflexible one, barbaric even. The rites of passage involve pain—some might call it torture. You know how they armor themselves." He glanced at her for affirmation, and she nodded.

"When they are initiated—the scarring process—they must not armor themselves—something, I am sure, that takes a great deal of self-discipline. And it's not just a one-time thing, as I'm sure you can imagine from the extent of the scarring."

Fissa nodded again, her throat now tight and dry. She hadn't even guessed at what was involved; she'd assumed it wouldn't hurt because he wouldn't let it.

"Koss' ship was crippled during a run-in with the Combine. It landed on Ferenc's planet for repairs. Ferenc befriended them; he possesses, among other things, a curiosity not shared by his people. Strangers are forbidden there." He paused as Fissa gave him an odd smile, thinking, You don't know the half of it.

"They turned on him," he continued after a polite and expectant wait, "and he escaped with Koss and his crew—most of them anyway. The ship limped on to the nearest planet, but required extensive repairs. That's why they were on the St. Catherine. I learned this from the two bodyguards left behind."

That gave him something to sink his teeth into, she thought. "Then you can't send him back," she said, not wanting to sound too eager.

The captain agreed.

"What are you going to do with him?"

He was silent for a minute, and she was afraid he wasn't going to tell her anything. Then, "I've been in touch with someone who may find him and his peculiar abilities useful," he said.

"Useful," she breathed through clenched teeth. "Useful, how?!"

He shrugged, stood, and she knew she'd learned all she was going to from him. She went straight to the purser's office to learn from Fortsworth where Koss' rooms were, but he warned her she wouldn't be allowed access.

She spent the last night before making planetfall on Mozartt, brooding in her room, wondering what to do next. She hadn't really expected to reach Ferenc, but she was bewildered because he hadn't come to her. She was sure that if he wanted to, he could.

The door chimed, squawked actually, and she activated it immediately. It was Ferenc; she hurriedly pulled him inside. "Does anyone know you're here?" she asked. She needed to find out if he had come or been sent.

"No. It is necessary that you understand what I have done—to you."

That stopped her in her tracks, and just when she'd gotten up the courage to wrap herself around him. "Tell me," she urged, draping herself instead seductively on the bed. He looked at her, momentarily teetering before getting himself under control. She almost expected him to armor himself, just to be on the safe side.

He was tense, strung tighter than she'd ever seen him—or rather, as she'd never seen him. He was afraid, she realized with a start, and she began to be a little nervous herself.

"You will have two sons."

"Is this some sort of prediction?" She'd left the seductive position and was now on her hands and knees on the bed, facing him, lips drawn not quite all the way back yet.

"It will happen." He appeared more relaxed since his confession—or perhaps from the fact she hadn't torn his throat out.

"Not necessarily," she hissed. From his calm demeanor she guessed he didn't have a clue as to what she meant. Not that she really meant it. She'd certainly never expected to find herself in this position—just like every other woman faced with this millennia-old dilemma, she thought bitterly.

But it was a little late for protestations. The need now was to plan for the future. To do that, she'd better learn more about his past. "What exactly happens on your planet between a man and a woman, Ferenc? I need to know."

He was clearly reluctant to discuss it, so she lay down again on the bed, invitingly, in an attempt to remind him... She hoped he would come to her, but he didn't. Instead, he started speaking.

"Men and women live apart," he said, "and when it is time, the man finds a woman, and if she is willing, they share water. She will not fight him then. A woman's bite leaves a scar that will not heal, it is said. Then they separate."

"The water is both a tranquilizer and an aphrodisiac?"

"Yes."

He'd probably learned both those words from Koss, Fissa figured. "What happens then—to us?" she demanded.

"You care for the cubs, and when they are old enough, they go to be men."

Cubs! Who taught him that? she wondered. The more she learned of his planet, the more she understood why it was proscribed. "You are not planning to take them to your planet, are you?" She kept her tone level.

"No," he said, but he sounded uncertain. He hadn't really thought about it, she realized. Natural enough. On his planet the rules were so rockbound, the lines so sharply drawn, there was very little need to think.

Right now she felt a little rockhard herself. The only thing she was sure of was that he would not get his hands on the children. He shifted, glancing at the door and escape.

"Coward," she said softly. He stiffened and in a second was at her side. It worked. She'd not only been sure he'd know the word, but how he'd react to it.

"Why do you call me coward?" he demanded.

"Here," she said, "a man is responsible for his children and his...woman. You are abandoning me to the scorn of my family, my tribe, my people." He was bound to recognize one of those words.

"What do you want me to do?"

So simple it was, and so hard. She slipped off the bed and stood up, biting the inside of her mouth, striving not to break down. "Here, when a man wants, or takes, a woman, there is a ceremony called marriage." She wouldn't go on to explain or to beg.

"There is no need for marriage now, I thought," he said slowly. He'd learned that from Koss, she guessed.

"There are those who do not bother," she added, putting all the contempt and loathing she could into it, loading each word with ice-cold emphasis.

She could see he was considering what she said, turning it over slowly in his mind, and examining it. She felt hopeful; it seemed as if he might actually like the idea. "Yes," he said at last.

It wasn't what she dreamed of when still a romantic young maid, but it would do—for now. "Do not say anything to the captain," she cautioned, while scrambling for a more viable plan. "You are going to meet a man on Mozartt, the captain told me. What has he told you?"

"There is a man who might find me useful, as Koss did," he replied.

"Not like Koss, I hope," she said sharply. "You must tell this man you will not work for him unless he can arrange for us to be married. Insist on it. You have that right, and you have the right to time off—to see me and the twins. If they don't let you come to Wodenhouse, you must send me word."

"I will come," he promised, and then he said, "twins?"

"The two boys," she said, and, impelled by a recently learned caution, went on to explain: "When two children are born together, they are called twins."

"But they will not be born together."

"Impossible," but it was a feeble protest. She rallied. "That may be true with your people, but it doesn't work that way with us." That sounded almost positive; but inside, she was close to gibbering.

The next morning before she disembarked, she said her good-byes and thank yous to the crew, especially Snark and Fortsworth. Then she went to see the captain.

"I'm sorry you are leaving us, Anfissa," he said. "I had thought you were enjoying your trip on the St. Catherine. Are you so easily frightened that you must return to the safety of your home and your mother?" Although his tone was polite, she couldn't miss the fact that he was disappointed in her. It even sounded as if he would miss her. Still, he was a man easily bored, and that reminded her.

"It's a pity," she said as she stood up, "that Old Nordic will get away with the havoc he wreaked on us all."

His hard green eyes softened a bit as he stared at her, and almost purring he said, "It would be a pity, wouldn't it?" She thought he watched her fondly as she turned to go.

From the ship, she went straight to the closest port hotel to wait, but when she registered, the clerk handed her a message tape. She activated it in the privacy of her room. "Major Roncador is waiting for you at headquarters. A car will collect you immediately."

What car and what headquarters? As she pondered, her room comm chimed. "Your car is here, Miss Skarvan," the desk clerk said. So much for the bath.

She took the express elevator up to ground level. The only car out front was a nondescript wreck of a skimmer, obviously left over from a battle—understandable when you knew that Mozartt's name was an acronym for Mercenary Organizations—all Zones—and Armed Response Tactical Teams.

The skimmer's driver was young and had only one arm and got Fissa to the headquarters building on the opposite side of the port without once slowing down. It didn't even stop when they approached the building; instead it sped through an irising door, cut power, and dropped into a shaft. They didn't waste time or take chances on this planet.

The skimmer parked in front of a cargo-sized door, and the driver herded her through a short, narrow corridor past plastisteel-shuttered offices and delivered her to an older, tired-looking man who turned from a bank of monitors to consider her. "You want to be married, I understand?"

"Yes."

"Ferenc says he will not serve me unless I help you two get married. He's adamant about that, referring all questions to you. I'm afraid he doesn't understand the concept of enlistment yet."

Fissa stiffened. "Has he enlisted?" she said sharply. "Just what do you plan to do with him anyway?" Adamant! She'd show them adamant. Incensed, she thought that if she could just get to him, they'd escape.

"We don't plan to waste him, if that's what you're worried about. We're not putting him in the front lines; we're going to use him in undercover operations; and that's classified, too." He scowled at her.

Fissa relaxed a little. "I can keep a secret," she said.

He studied her for a moment, then nodded. "I wonder if Captain Saknusson knew what you were planning."

"My family would not approve of this marriage," she said. "I hope you're not worried by that." She tried to inject just the right combination of query and contempt into her voice.

"Manipulative little minx, aren't you?" he said with open admiration. "No, it doesn't worry me. As a matter of fact, it would be a very good idea to keep this under wraps. By the way, are you planning to change your name when you marry?"

"No." Actually, she hadn't even considered it. "We always keep our own names," she said, this time cheerfully tossing in a pinch of superciliousness.

"Good. It's safer that way. Now, do you have a preference as to a marriage ceremony? We have an assortment of priests, parsons, rabbis, and even a twiner on planet. I'm afraid I can only allow you a week for a honeymoon. Afterwards, where do you plan to stay? Your family estate on Wodenhouse would be safest, of course."

A week. She hadn't hoped for that, but now that she thought about it, she saw it would be not only a good thing, but essential. Aloud, she said, "Why do you keep harping on safety?"

"Ferenc's extremely fortunate to be surrounded by protective people. But there are others who'd see him only as a valuable commodity—useful in various violent and illegal undertakings. He, and possibly his progeny, have to be safeguarded." He regarded her impatiently. "Now, about the wedding."

Momentarily speechless, Fissa stared at him until his tapping fingers forced her to concentrate. "It doesn't really matter," she said.

He hit a button. "The Padre," he said, before looking up at her. "He's trustworthy."

###

The wedding was as quiet and secret as Fissa could have wished for. Major Roncador and the driver, Kyle Madden, whose name she only learned when she saw it on the wedding certificate she insisted upon procuring, were the only witnesses.

"You'll want somewhere private and safe," Roncador told them as soon as the minister stopped speaking. "I'm lending you my bungalow deep in the hills. I usually sleep here anyway. Kyle'll drive you there."

"Thank you, Major," Fissa said, with heartfelt gratitude. He nodded absently as he turned away, already concentrating on the next problem.

Kyle flew them out to the hills in a different car. "It's the major's," he explained. Naturally, and of course the windows were darkened so no one could see it wasn't the major.

The bungalow, literally buried, not picturesquely, in the hills, was a cozy place. Though sparsely furnished, it had all they needed—a bed and plenty of food and water.

Fissa worked hard at persuading Ferenc that they didn't need to share water to make love, though it wasn't as hard as she feared since he'd gotten a taste of it on Snakebite. She also got him to promise there would be no more children without her consent; she suspected this method had evolved so that men and women didn't have to spend too much time together.

The week was sheer pleasure, enhanced by the comfort of a soft bed and safety; and Ferenc was eager to learn more about Fissa and the planet where his sons would be raised. She wasn't able to learn anything about how she was expected to care for the boys, nor what he planned to do with them. The first was her business, and the latter was his, so she refrained from enlightening him about her own plans.

From all she'd learned, Fissa was sure Ferenc enjoyed being with her more than was normal among his people, but she wondered if he would miss her at all afterwards. She frequently told him she loved him, even though she was afraid it didn't mean anything to him. Love apparently didn't figure much in sex and relationships on his planet. If he came back to her, it would probably be because of his sons.

At the end of the week, the comm chimed. "The major's car will be here in an hour," it told them. It was early, and still in bed Fissa looked at Ferenc. Whether or not he read the regret in her eyes, he knelt next to her, gathered her in his arms, and loved her as wholeheartedly as she desired. He no longer worried about her attacking him when they made love, and she hoped their last hour was as precious to him as it was to her. She knew that in the presence of other people, he wouldn't come near her.

She packed after the car arrived. The major had driven out himself, and he and Ferenc left her alone to do it. Though they'd doubtless been discussing Ferenc's future, Roncador talked only of generalities on the trip back to the port. He dropped her off at the same hotel she'd stayed at so briefly, and she contented herself with a brief touch of her lips on Ferenc's cheek as she got out. He turned slightly towards her before catching himself.

From the desk clerk Fissa got a list of outgoing ships and their destinations. She would have preferred the St. Catherine, but it would be easier travelling on a ship where no one knew her. Studying the list, she decided to take the long way home.

Four months later, uncertain as to how far along she was, but starting to show, she arrived on Wodenhouse. She was surprised at how good it felt seeing the full-scale Viking ship in the center of the port welcome center and having a car from the estate awaiting her out front.

The estate was large, covering almost an eighth of the planet, but it contained a number of households. Skarvan Hold was one of three family estates that still held all the land granted them when the planet was colonized. The family held hard to their Viking heritage as well. The only reason they'd named the planet Wodenhouse was because Odin was taken.

Amazing how you appreciate things so much more when you return to them—things like home and Mother, who stood, serene and tall, the thick blond, braided hair crowning her head making her look even taller. Fissa rushed to hug her, the memory of her departure and rebellious words disappearing like wisps of mist.

"Welcome home, Anfissa," her mother murmured as she stroked Fissa's hair, holding her tight until Fissa pushed away and stepped back.

"I'm only back for a visit, Mother," Fissa said as they climbed the wide, rounded steps leading to the house.

Toria Skarvan nodded, then paused inside the portico. "How long?"

Fissa bit her lower lip, wondering just how her mother meant that.

When she didn't answer, her mother continued, "I have arranged, if you wish, for you to have a place of your own. There are two available—one on the water, the other in the woods, though that one is just down the road from here.'"

Fissa looked up at the massive white building towering above. It was deep and long, with a large round tower at each end; she'd feel safer inside its stalwart walls. It was the oldest building on Skarvan Hold, built like a fortress and modeled after an old Swedish castle. "Here, I think, for now," she said.

Fissa was surprised and touched when her mother gave her the North Tower suite. Her Uncle Torvil had the South Tower. Her mother even respected her privacy, so that Fissa had to seek her out when she finally decided to talk to her.

"Then he said I would have two sons, but not at the same time." Toria Skarvan, her blue eyes intense, listened without a single interruption. Speechless with shock, Fissa suspected.

"It sounds as if he is very different from us," her mother said finally, "physically I mean. I think you should have a very thorough checkup."

Fissa shook her head. "I've thought about that. We don't know how early a baby can armor itself. What if a scan or a simple probe startles it? What will happen to me? For all we know, their women have cast iron tummies. Mother, I'm afraid."

This time Toria Skarvan seemed genuinely shocked. "You may be right; we'll have to talk to a specialist. You've left it a little late, you know."

"I know. I've thought about that too. I want these babies," she said, forgiving her mother the worried rebuke.

Toria left her chair. Kneeling beside Fissa, she took her hand and said, "If that's what you want, you know I'll help you however I can."

Usually, in such a position, Fissa felt small—and young. But now, she was doing the reassuring. "I'm not really worried, Mother. Ferenc would never do anything to hurt me. It's just that sometimes—not knowing..."

Fissa passed the time studying her heritage—on Wodenhouse and on Terra, children—the birth and care of, missing and worrying about Ferenc, and in thinking up names.

"I'm almost positive that Eirik and Petek are the ones. They sound similar to Ferenc and yet they're ours. Of course, I wouldn't be surprised if, on his planet, the names the women give their children are discarded, and the fathers choose new ones for them. But that's not going to happen here."

Toria Skarvan looked up, dropping the tangled knitting into her lap. With a faint sigh of relief, she said, "Wise decision, that. Not taking up knitting little booties for you was, too. I don't know what possessed me to attempt it again."

"Some primitive maternal instinct, but..." She glanced down at her body. It reminded her of an ungainly sea creature on Terra she'd recently learned about. "I can see why you only had one child," she continued fretfully.

Toria smiled. "Like you, I wanted adventure. Hendryk and I went aroving a lot as a matter of fact. Even after I married your father, I resisted having a child for as long as I could. Not that having you slowed me down much. I traveled everywhere with your father. When he died, I had to spend more time at the Hold, and you were getting to be quite a handful. All you remember is having me here."

Fissa had never thought of her mother having a life, let alone an interesting one. "You and Captain Saknusson?!" she said in astonishment, and went on to ask, "Why is he captaining the St. Catherine? From what I learned, he'd rather be doing more exciting things."

"The St. Catherine is part of his inheritance; his brother Howald has several cargo ships. Hendryk's done many different things with that ship. He always said it was the next best thing to being a sea captain." For just an instant her mother looked regretful.

Suddenly Fissa felt guilty. "I'm sorry, Mother," she said.

Toria looked at her. "Don't be silly. You are the most precious thing in my life," she said.

They sat silently for a while, until Fissa said, "I'm hungry."

###

A week later, Fissa was on her way to the kitchen again. She'd been worrying about whether she was absorbing all the nutrients her child needed, whether he might need something available only on his native planet. Suddenly she felt a contraction.

Resisting the overwhelming desire to stand there and shriek, "Mother!" she made her way steadily to the room prepared for the birthing, and hit the broadcast switch on the room's comm. "It's time," she announced. Then she lowered herself gingerly onto the bed and waited for the midwife and her mother to come. Toria had also arranged for two doctors to be nearby.

Toria arrived first. Pale but calm, she went to Fissa's side. "How do you feel?" she asked with maternal concern, before turning to the comm and yelling, "Marta!"

Even as the imperative call echoed throughout the room, Marta was on her way in. Though not much taller than Toria, the broad woman bustled. "No need to panic," she told them soothingly as she busied herself rearranging Fissa and her bed, gently moving Toria out of the way.

"Stay, Mother," Fissa begged.

"Of course. Now just relax."

"Yes," Fissa said, remembering. It's all right, she said to herself and to her child, or was it childs? She wished she knew. She wished it was over. How long does this go on?! It seemed like forever. Come on out, she thought, catching herself up. It's all right, you can come out NOW!

"That's a good girl," Marta said. "Just keep pushing. Aaah, here it comes."

Fissa looked up at her mother, who was tenderly wiping her wet face. SWAACK!

"No!" Fissa yelped, and her mother leaped for the baby, grabbed, and wrapped it quickly.

Marta looked puzzled. "Something happened," she said slowly. "You'd better let me look at it."

"No," said Fissa and her mother simultaneously.

"It's just his Viking blood," Toria said. "He probably resented being slapped. I'll take care of him. You see to Anfissa." And she took the baby from the room.

"His father's from off-planet, I think?" Marta ventured.

"Yes," Fissa said. There was no point in denying it.

Marta grunted. She would have liked to learn more, but one of the things a midwife learns is discretion.

###

Over nine months later, Fissa glanced down at her swollen stomach and sighed. She couldn't decide if she looked more like a walrus or a whale. At least Ferenc had never seen her like this. She frowned in irritation. Well, serve him right if he did. But probably he wouldn't show up until it was time for boys to become men.

"At least you're not as worried this time," her mother said sympathetically. Fissa looked up and squirmed, trying to find a more comfortable position.

She had to agree. "No, but trained sperm? Who would have believed it? I wonder where it hid itself. Sometimes I wish I'd had twins, but I probably would have exploded, and they'd have been born halfway around the planet."

Toria smiled. "I think it is better this way. Eirik is still asleep, by the way."

"Thanks, Mother. Where's Marta?"

"Not far away. I can still picture her when she arrived last week: how she gave you that searching look, and made that little humming grunt which means she's not going to say a word, then went for a walk in the woods. When she starts hovering, we go inside."

Fissa nodded. Until then, she'd sit out here in the sun. It was a craving almost as strong as the one she'd had for sparkleberries and tomato juice. She and her mother had discussed it and decided it must be important.

Toria leaned back in her chair. "I have two doctors on standby again. They're in the house in the woods, probably still wondering how they ended up spending their vacation here."

Fissa smiled up at the sky. "You're a marvel, Mother" she said. "By the way, Marta wanted to see little Eirik so I escorted her to the nursery. Freki kept watch, staying right by the bed. She said, 'Good woofie.' If she wondered why we have a guard beast, she didn't ask."

"She wouldn't. Some people aren't curious, but she is and manages to contain it. Not an easy feat. And speaking of curious people, I'm adding more sensors along the sea cliffs, and Hendryk's getting me some heavy artillery, just in case. He didn't ask why either, but he wanted to," she said with a pronounced air of satisfaction.

Fissa nodded. It didn't seem likely they'd need them, but ... but... Yes. That was definitely a spasm. "Mother, maybe we should go in now." Toria whipped out of her chair and helped Fissa get up. That was one reason why she was out here.

Marta met them at the door. Obviously she'd been watching. Now she bustled them both into the birthing room and helped Fissa lie down. "I'm not worried this time, Mother," Fissa said, just before grabbing her mother's hand, hard.

This time it went faster and easier, and Marta didn't try to hit Petek, though Toria kept a watchful eye on her, once again taking charge of the newborn.

"That was even quicker than the first one," Marta said, allowing only a touch of wonder in her voice. Fissa was grateful that Marta didn't ask questions, like Where was the father? and Why did they need a genetically engineered guard dog in a place as remote and well-protected as Skarvan Hold?

Eight months later Fissa and her mother were relaxing on a blanket, on the sun-bright expanse of moss green lawn that spread out from the house and down to the woods. "It won't be long before Petek's walking," Toria said, watching Petek clutching Freki's ruff. His little feet only occasionally touched the ground as the black and silver hybrid paced back and forth at the edge of the blanket, keeping a watchful eye on Eirik, who was halfway to the trees.

"It's too bad we can't get another one for Petek," Fissa said. Guard beasts arrived in stasis with imprinting instructions, but the same qualities that made them such perfect guardians also made them view others of their kind as threats.

"Excuse me, Lady Toria."

"What is it, Sondra?" Toria glanced up at the housemaid.

"There was a call," Sondra explained. "He asked if Ferenc was here. I didn't know exactly who he meant." Actually she'd heard the others discussing him, but there was no official word. "I said I'd have to ask, but he cut the transmission."

Toria looked at Eirik and hesitated. She worked hard at not telling Fissa what to do about the children. Fissa glanced at her mother, saw the struggle written plainly on her face and laughed. "I'll call..."

Then they heard the alarms that meant an incoming vehicle.

"Take Petek inside!" Toria screamed. "I'll get Eirik." She reached under the blanket and pulled out her laser rifle, just as the aircar plummeted from the sky and hit the ground with an earth-shattering thud. Too fast for the automatic weapons.

Fissa was already running back with Petek. A man swung out of the car behind her, but Toria changed his mind with a shot that crisped the grass at his feet and another that singed his arm. He jumped back inside, and Fissa tore past her mother into the house. "I sent Freki to Eirik," she gasped.

Toria nodded. "Stay in the house!" she commanded. Fissa watched, the front door ajar, as her mother headed straight for the car, using it for cover. Then she disappeared behind the back of the car.

Fissa, clutching Petek's hand tightly with one hand, and the edge of the door with the other, got ready to slam it shut while berating herself for not being armed. She'd left it to her mother. Then she felt her hand being firmly disengaged. "Hang on to this," said a raspy voice. Looming over her was Uncle Torvil. He shoved a gun into her hand.

Sondra popped up behind him. "Everyone else was busy barricading, so I went up and got him."

"Think I didn't hear the alarms?" the old man muttered resentfully. If his remaining ear wasn't as good as it used to be, his blue eyes were still bright and alert, and one, large hairy fist carelessly wielded one of the guns mounted in the towers. He'd brought it with him from his rooms.

Then came the screaming, abruptly cut short. Fissa whirled back to the door and would have yanked it open, but Torvil braced himself against it firmly, shoving her back. "Stay," he said before going outside.

Just like before, Fissa thought. Telling her what to do. Then she felt Petek's hand in hers, his other clutching her long skirt. Picking him up, she settled him on her hip and looked out the door, gun at the ready. If she had to, she'd have Sondra take him to the cellars, and she'd go out, too. Waiting, watching, she saw her mother come around the front of the car, carrying Eirik.

Giving Petek to Sondra, she hurried out to meet her mother. "Where's Uncle Torvil and Freki?"

Toria handed Eirik over. "Torvil's taking care of Freki. We'll need a stretcher. One of the men practically blew his leg off. I beamed his gun; it exploded and put him out of action, so I could concentrate on the other one, who was getting too close." With a rueful smile, she indicated her frizzled hair. Fissa was shocked to see the high-piled braids had almost disappeared.

"It's a good thing you wear your hair up, Mother. It probably caused him to aim high," Fissa said, wrenching her gaze from the remains of the hair with great effort.

Toria shrugged. "The pilot couldn't decide whether to leave or join the fray; he wasted too much time on the decision. I wasn't about to let him go. In the meantime, Freki dragged himself to the man I wounded. I suppose you heard him scream; there was nothing I could do. I did want to question him," she said with regret.

Fissa started for the house. "I'll get some men with a stretcher. You sound the all clear and call the vet."

"There's something more," Toria said, easily keeping pace as Fissa hurried back. "Eirik armored himself, I believe you call it, and he was going to help Freki. I'm really looking forward to meeting his father," she added.

The vet arrived less than a half hour after they called. "I'll have to take off what's left of his leg," he told them. "He's not going to be much use to you, though. So, if you want me to put him down so you can get another one..." Continuing to stroke the unconscious animal, he waited for their decision.

"I can't, Mother, not Freki." She looked down at the wolf-like hybrid. She'd had a choice among the wolf types; or the big cats, bred and engineered as climbers and jumpers; or slightly scaled-down gorillas; and something like octopi, useful on water planets. But she liked the wolves, and she loved Freki.

Her mother reached out and patted Freki's head. "I agree. Freki's one of us. We'll take care of him, too."

The vet smiled with relief. "There're some who'll put an animal down when they get tired of it," he said. They left while he and his robotic assistant set up the lights and equipment.

Two weeks later, Freki got up from his blanket on the front lawn; stiff but determined, he moved off to join Eirik and Petek. The two women watched to be sure the wolf didn't over-exert himself on his first day out of the house, but the two boys had almost instinctively made allowances for him and stayed close.

Fissa was drowsing in the sun, fairly confident none of them would stray too far, when the alarm went off. She rolled over, reached, and both she and her mother came up with their weapons ready. "House, boys!" she said.

"The woods. Something's broken through the barrier by the sound of it," Toria said, as Eirik and Petek headed obediently towards the house.

"I'll bring Freki," Fissa said.

But, when she tried to bring him in, he refused. Standing stubbornly on three legs, he faced the wood behind the house and tested the air; then, slowly, his tail began to wag. That certainly didn't indicate danger, but what could he possibly recognize, unless it was something that smelled like the boys?

Head up in unconscious imitation of Freki, Fissa faced the wood. Again unconsciously, she moved forward a couple steps, torn between retreating to safety and hoping...

Then someone stepped out from the wood. As soon as he left the shadows cast by the trees spread high and thick behind him, he appeared golden in the strong light of Wodenhouse's sun. Fissa, lingering no longer, went straight to meet him.

"Welcome home," she said, refusing to dwell on why he'd come. For now it was enough to hold him close. To her delight, he responded instantly, wrapping his arms around her in turn; and when she lifted her head to look, his face had softened to golden-brown.

"Have you come to see your sons?" she dared to ask at last, drawing away and watching him closely.

Caressing her cheek with a finger, he smiled. "I've come to you," he said, pulling her to him and kissing her. She remembered his touch, his kiss, forgetting everything else until she felt a heavy, warm body leaning against her leg and she heard her mother's voice.

"This must be Ferenc," Toria said pleasantly. "Why don't you bring him in, Fissa, and Freki, too. He needs to rest."

Toria's tone seemed perfectly natural, but Fissa suspected she'd been afraid her errant daughter had been about to make love on the lawn. She knelt beside Freki and hid her blushing face in his coat for a second before looking up at Ferenc. "This is Freki," she said. "He lost his leg protecting us."

Ferenc dropped down in front of the guard beast and took the huge head in his hands. Fissa found herself wondering whether relations between men and animals on Ferenc's planet were better or worse than between its people.

She was relieved when Ferenc gathered Freki in his arms, got up, and headed for the house, she and Toria following close behind. The doors stood open, with Torvil on guard on the steps, his gun hanging loosely at his side. He stepped back to let them pass.

In the presence of the others, Ferenc kept his hands to himself, rarely looking at her. It made her impatient—she wanted him to herself. But, the first thing she did was introduce him to their sons.

"Eirik is the oldest," she said, her hands on the boy's shoulders as she escorted him to his father. She picked Petek up and sat with him in her lap, on the floor at Ferenc's feet. "And this is Petek. I hope you're pleased with them." Protectively, she held the boys close, her eyes daring him to find fault with them.

"I am pleased," he said, his eyes resting on her for a long moment as they took on a familiar glow.

Supper was meant to be a celebration, but Fissa wanted only to be finished with it; so as soon as they were done, she went to her mother. "Ferenc and I are going to my rooms now. We need to talk." It was a difficult thing to say, since she knew her mother wasn't stupid.

"Of course," Toria said. "I'll put the boys to bed."

"Thank you, Mother." Fissa started toward Ferenc, but turned back to add, firmly. "We'll need a place of our own now."

"Of course." In a gesture very like Fissa's, she bit her lower lip thoughtfully. "Perhaps you would like to build. If it's true that Ferenc can't go home again, he may want to incorporate some things that mean home to him."

"Bless you, Mother. I never thought of that. So often I don't think about how things are for him," she said in self-reproach.

"You two have already learned more about each other than most couples ever will. I'm proud of you, and Hendryk has told me how much he admires you. He's on his way to Wodenhouse," she added. "He wants to talk to you. He called just before I went out to get you. He wants you to call him—something about closing the trap on Old Nordic," she added curiously.

Fissa gave her mother a pleading look. "Not tonight. Can't you tell him I'll call tomorrow?"

Toria laughed. "I'll find out what he wants," she promised.

Fissa said good-night to Eirik, Petek, and her uncle. As she swung around behind the vu-phone, she heard her mother say, "I know I've been stuck on Wodenhouse a long time, but I wouldn't call it stagnating. Come by tomorrow, and we'll talk about what we've been doing. In any case, I can help you with Old Nordic as well as Fissa can." She cut the transmission. Fissa stopped dead and stared at her mother.

"Mother, I don't think you should."

Toria, raising her eyebrows, glanced across the room. "Ferenc's waiting," she said. Then she gave Fissa a wicked grin and quoted, " 'I can take care of myself. You never let me off this planet!' "

Fissa laughed ruefully, kissed her mother, and joined Ferenc. As they climbed the tower stairs, Fissa remembered something her mother used to say: "Family comes first." She knew now what she meant, but couldn't she, couldn't they... ?

The End

About the author:

Joy V. Smith has been writing stories since she was a kid. Her stories, articles, and interviews have been published in print magazines, webzines, and anthologies; and her SF has been published in two audiobooks, including *Sugar Time*. Recent books include *Building a Cool House for Hot Times without Scorching the Pocketbook*, a children's picture book, *Why Won't Anyone Play with Me?*, and an ebook, *Remodeling: Buying and Updating a Foreclosure*, which is also available on Smashwords. She lives in Florida with Blizzard the Snow Princess and Bryn the Flying Corgi.

Check out her media blog at: **http://pagadan.livejournal.com/**

Also by Joy V. Smith

Lori and Chiing
Pretty Pink Planet
Hot Yellow Planet

Standalone
Remodeling: Buying and Updating a Foreclosure
Hidebound
Velvet of Swords
Well Met by Water
Seedlings
Crystal Quest

Watch for more at www.joyvsmith.com.

About the Author

Joy V. Smith has been writing stories since she was a kid and made her own little books. She went to the University of Wisconsin-Oshkosh, where she received a BA in English--and probably spent more time writing--and reading.-- than studying. She has written short stories and articles--including interviews with editors, artists, and writers. She actually began writing novels when she discovered NaNoWriMo.

Along the way she also built a house, and so she wrote a non-fiction book, Building a Cool House for Hot Times without Scorching the Pocketbook. Some years later she downsized. She remodeled the next house--and wrote a book about that. She focuses on her science fiction novels though.

Read more at www.joyvsmith.com.